Griffin Rising

By Darby Karchut

Twilight Times Books
Kingsport Tennessee

Griffin Rising

This is a work of fiction. All concepts, characters and events portrayed in this book are used fictitiously and any resemblance to real people or events is purely coincidental.

Paladin Timeless Books, an imprint of
Twilight Times Books
P O Box 3340
Kingsport TN 37664
http://twilighttimesbooks.com/

First Edition, June 2011

Library of Congress Cataloging-in-Publication Data

Karchut, Darby.
Griffin rising / by Darby Karchut. -- 1st ed.
p. cm.
Summary: Armed with the power to control the ancient elements of Earth and Fire, sixteen year old Griffin is determined to complete his apprenticeship and rise to the rank of Terrae Angeli, but first, he must overcome a brutal past in order to survive in this world.
ISBN-13: 978-1-60619-210-8 (trade pbk. : alk. paper)
ISBN-10: 1-60619-210-8 (trade pbk. : alk. paper)
[1. Angels--Fiction. 2. Apprentices--Fiction. 3. Supernatural--Fiction.] I. Title.
PZ7.K133Gr 2011
[Fic]--dc22

2011000057

Cover art by Ardy M. Scott

Printed in the United States of America.

To Wes, my terra firma
as well as my terrae angelus.

The Manuscript of Aidan, Abbot of Kellsfarne
In the Year of Our Lord 1144

Of all spiritual beings, Angels are most sublime. As far as the heavens are above the earth, Angels are above all other spirits. They are reflections of the Divine Thinker and exist to do His bidding alone. As Messengers and Warriors, they are peerless. Nine choirs there are of Angels: Seraphim, Cherubim, Thrones, the Virtues, the Powers, the Dominions, Principalities, Archangels, and Angels.

However, there exist other spiritual beings, of which we know little. Rumors abound of a lowly caste known as the Terrae Angeli. *A dim shadow of Heavenly Angelic powers and strengths,* Terrae Angeli *exist only to serve as guardians to man. Four ranks have they: Sage, Guardian, Mentor, and Tiro.*

This we know of Terrae Angeli:
Being earthbound, their powers are limited.
Being earthbound, they mirror man in all ways, even unto free will.
Being earthbound, their appearances and powers align to the Four Elements: Wind & Water, Earth & Fire.
Being earthbound, they can destroy and be destroyed.

Translation from the original Latin:
Professor Julian Fitzwilliam
Oxford
1898

Prologue

"UM ... BASIL?" SAID THE TEEN, pushing his dark hair out of his eyes. He glanced around the abandoned parking lot, its rotting blacktop camouflaged by a layer of snow, then looked up at his tall companion. "I think your pant leg's on fire." Gesturing toward his Mentor's foot, he added, "in case you were wondering about that burnt denim smell."

"By the Light, Griffin!" Basil took a hasty step back and looked down. Grumbling under his breath, he leaned over and pointed his fingers, Water spraying from the tips of his fingers like miniature fire extinguishers. "And precisely how many times have I told you—no Elements during flight?" Steam rose with a hiss from his cuff as he waved his hand back and forth.

"I'm guessing the low hundreds?" Griffin smiled sheepishly as he dug in his pocket and pulled out his phone.

"Yet here I am. All ablaze. Again." After a few moments, Basil straightened up. He wiped his fingers dry on his jeans, then ran a hand through his cropped white hair. "And I'd suggest you put *that* away and start warming up. You haven't much time."

"Just checking," he said, scrolling down. "Katie said she'd try to leave me a message for luck between classes." He snapped it shut and handed it over. "Would you hold this for me?" Stepping away, he rolled his shoulders, then took a deep breath and dropped to one knee; cocking his arm back, he punched his fist into the ground. With a rumble, the pavement shuddered and rippled outward, forming a ring of broken asphalt around him, the jagged tips poking up through the snow like black teeth. "How's that for control?" He glanced up at his Mentor as he rose, blowing on his smarting knuckles.

"Better," said Basil. "Speaking of Katie—she seems to have adapted fairly well to who and what you are."

Griffin nodded, then lifted his arm and pointed toward the far corner. A ribbon of Fire erupted from his forefinger in a roar. With the fiery ink, he wrote his name across the snow-covered lot, the giant letters glowing in the dim light of the overcast afternoon. They faded, leaving a slushy signature.

"You know, human guys do that by—" Griffin began, then stopped when Basil raised a hand in protest.

"I'm well aware of certain ... *rituals* ... performed by male adolescents."

Griffin grinned at his Mentor's expression, his brown eyes crinkling at the corners. "Anyway, Katie's totally cool about me. After all," he said, beaming, "I *am* an angel. Well, an angel of a lesser sort," he added. "The perfect boyfriend." They both chuckled, grateful for the laughter keeping their fears at bay. After a moment, Griffin's smile faded as he studied the isolated warehouse, its metal siding rattling in the wind.

"Basil?"

"Fin."

"I *so* don't want to do this." He licked his lips nervously.

"I know, lad."

They stood in silence for a few minutes, the wind mixing with sleet as it swirled around them, ruffling Griffin's hair. Then he sighed and lifted his chin. "Well, here goes nothing," he said and started for the door.

"A moment, please." Basil reached out and snagged the hood of his apprentice's sweatshirt, yanking him back. "I want a final word with you."

"Stop doing that!" Griffin tugged it back into place.

"But it's such a convenient leash," said Basil. He sighed and stepped forward, placing a hand on one of Griffin's sturdy shoulders. I can't believe he's sixteen earth years already, the Mentor thought, and facing this trial by combat.

Along with the monster who still haunts his nightmares.

Basil cleared his throat. "Speed is your best tactic, my young Tiro," he began, his blue eyes intense. "And you *are* wicked fast." A corner of Griffin's mouth twitched at the rare praise. "The sooner you break the circle, the better. Do not give Nicopolis time to get the upper hand." He let go as Griffin nodded, shuffling his feet. "And remember—"

"I know. I know. All your other Tiros passed theirs, so I better not be the first one to fail *my* Proelium and embarrass you," Griffin said. A nervous grin flashed across his face.

Basil snorted. "Cheeky," he said, affectionately cuffing him on the side of the head. "No. What I was about to say is that we've spent the last three years practicing every skill and strategy you need for this ordeal. So believe in yourself." He stepped back, gesturing toward the building. "Godspeed, Fin. I'll meet you here afterwards. And, by the way, kick Nicopolis' butt for *me*, would you?"

The young angel chuckled and gave a nod, then turned around, squaring his shoulders as he started toward the warehouse. With a faint smile still on his face, Griffin went into battle.

Three years earlier…

Chapter One

GRIFFIN GASPED AS HE STUMBLED ALONG, desperate to keep on his feet as Nicopolis dragged him up the sweeping driveway. He slipped again on the gravel, almost going down. Hunching his shoulders, he winced as the Mentor stopped and released the neck of his tee shirt long enough to clout him across the back of the head.

"Slow me down again, Tiro, and you'll not be able to walk for a week," said Nicopolis in a cold voice. As they neared the curved steps of the portico, he flung him to the ground.

Stifling a cry, Griffin crashed against a stone planter, the geraniums within shuddering from the impact. Petals drifted around him like red tears. Shaking his head, he rolled over, hands and feet scrabbling for purchase as the Mentor stalked toward him.

"I suggest you remain where you are." Nicopolis stared at him, his pale face unreadable. "But just to make sure ..." He stomped on one of Griffin's hands, pinning it to the ground.

Griffin cried out, writhing as he pushed against Nicopolis' wingtip shoe with his other hand, the raw gravel biting his palm. "Mentor! Please!"

Nicopolis shifted his weight. "Stop squirming and I'll ease off," he said, smoothing his lank hair across his forehead. He waited until Griffin froze, blinking back tears. "Before I do, however, let's chat about our latest mission, shall we?" He plucked a speck of lint off the front of his suit. "Another *unsuccessful* mission, I should say." With a smile, Nicopolis pressed harder.

"Stop—please stop!" begged Griffin. He grasped his own wrist, trying to pull free. "I'm sorry, Mentor. I'm sorry, I'm sorry!"

Nicopolis sniffed with disdain and stepped back, adjusting his tie as he circled Griffin. "Are you *deliberately* trying to tarnish my reputation? By failing mission after mission? Or are you truly this useless?" Griffin shook his head, a tear seeping into the corner of his mouth. "Well, it certainly appears that way." Nicopolis gestured with a flick of a bony finger. "Get up."

Griffin struggled to his feet and tucked his tender hand under an armpit. He tensed as Nicopolis leaned around and murmured in his ear.

"These last three years have been a complete waste of my time. I still cannot fathom why Command would give a Mentor of my status an apprentice like you." He shifted around to Griffin's other ear, his breath sour. "Tell me, Tiro. What happens if I decide to end your so-called apprenticeship?"

"I get kicked out," whispered Griffin.

"And?"

"And I become mortal."

Digging in with a squared nail, Nicopolis hooked a finger under Griffin's chin and forced him to look up. "Not the usual career goal for most Terrae Angeli, to be sure."

At least I'd be away from you, thought Griffin. His eyes flashed a brown fire.

Nicopolis raised an eyebrow. Without warning, he struck him across the face. Griffin staggered from the blow and then locked his knees, knowing the penalty for flinching.

"That was for disrespect." The Mentor gazed at him, head cocked to one side. "Now, where were we? Oh, yes. Your feeble attempts at ruining my status." He stepped back and pursed his lips. "It's high time we made some changes around here. I believe I'll contact Flight Command tomorrow. One worthless Tiro to dispose of." He turned on his heel and sauntered up the steps of the mansion, pausing at the entrance, one hand on the doorknob. Glancing over his shoulder, he added, "it's a pity I can't just leave you at the curb for pick-up. Along with the other rubbish." He snorted, and then disappeared inside.

After the massive doors had closed with a thud, Griffin sucked in a shuddering breath. Stretching out the sleeve of his tee shirt, he wiped his face, wincing from the sting of his cut lip, and then trudged toward the house; he made it as far as the lowest step before sinking down into a huddle. Tucking his hands between his knees and stomach, he stared at the ground, his face blank as he rocked back and forth.

Praying for the impossible.

ᘓᘗ

"Tiro."

Griffin flinched, banging his elbow on the inside of the bathtub, the scrub brush tumbling from his grasp; he lurched to his feet. "Yes, Mentor?"

Nicopolis sneered. "Must you be so ... well ... *you?*" He waited for a moment. "Sarcasm—it's wasted on the idiots," he said, shaking his head. "No matter—I have good news. I'm finally getting rid of you. In two days. Command actually found someone to take you. An old acquaintance of mine," he added, examining his appearance in the vanity mirror. "Mentor Basil."

Griffin's stomach lurched. An old acquaintance? His hand trembled as he reached for the brush again. He tightened his lips as he continued scrubbing, trying to swallow the fear rising in his throat.

ꙮ

Basil frowned in disbelief as he read the contents of the folder, unmindful of the morning sun pouring through the windows and slanting across his desk. He scribbled a few notes on the inside cover, then slapped it closed and tossed it on a stack of older files. What a complete muck-up, he thought, twirling the pen in his hand. What was Flight Command thinking when they placed him with Nicopolis? "They weren't bloody thinking," he said aloud, his English accent still distinct after centuries in the New World.

He checked his watch, stood up, and rummaged around the cluttered desktop for his car keys, finally locating them under his worn map of Colorado. Then he tucked in the tail of his shirt and crossed the hall, pausing to snatch his sports coat from the hook. Well, I best go rescue the lad.

ꙮ

His face twisted with frustration, Griffin rubbed at a stain on his shirt a few more times, then gave up. Stepping back, he studied himself in the cracked mirror. I look like the reject pile from a used clothing store, he thought. Wetting his fingers in the sink, he ran them through his hair, trying to smooth it down. Then he leaned closer to the mirror and examined the cut on his lip. I wish I could hide this. He sighed and stuck his mouth under the running faucet, trying to fill his empty stomach.

Wiping his chin, he glanced at the basement window at the rumble of a car pulling up to the front entrance. As the doorbell rang, he hitched up his jeans, grabbed his backpack by the knotted strap, and headed upstairs.

ℰ☙

Basil stepped out of his battered Saab and eyed the mansion with a shake of his head. A bit over the top for a guardian angel, he thought. But that's Nicopolis. It's always about appearances with him. He jogged up the stone steps two at a time, then rang the bell. After a long delay, the door opened. "Good morning, Nicopolis," he said as the other Mentor appeared. "I hope I'm not too early?"

"Not at all, Basil," replied Nicopolis, opening the door wider. "Won't you come in?" As Basil stepped into the soaring foyer, Nicopolis called over his shoulder, his voice echoing. "Come, Tiro!" He sighed as he turned back. "I apologize. He's never ... *anything.* Never on time. Never on task."

"Well, he *is* thirteen. A few missteps are to be expected from time to time."

"Not from my Tiros. I do not tolerate mistakes."

"Apparently not." They stared at each other in silence.

Nicopolis looked away first. "May I offer you something to drink? Tea?" he asked, gesturing toward the front parlor.

Basil shook his head. "Thank you, no. I'll just wait here." He stuffed his hands into his jean pockets, feet comfortably apart. His blue eyes flickered from the marble floor to the walls covered in elaborate mirrored panels.

"As you wish." Nicopolis pursed his lips. "So, I've heard a rumor that you still train your Tiros in the field. On actual missions?" he asked. "A bit old-fashioned, wouldn't you say?"

Basil shrugged. "I can't think of a better way to prepare young Terrae Angeli," he said. "Once they gain some experience, they're more of an asset than a liability."

Nicopolis snorted. "How you can stand to work with these useless cases is beyond me. Personally, I think we should cull them out at a younger age. And retain only the best ones."

They're not *puppies,* for heaven's sake, thought Basil as he struggled to keep the disgust off his face. "Not all Tiros fit the same pattern. All of my *useless cases* have gone on to become excellent guardians."

"Yes, yes, I'm sure they have," said Nicopolis and sniffed. "Basil, would you care for a friendly piece of advice? Mentor to Mentor?"

No, thought Basil. Not really.

"This one will never complete his apprenticeship. And he will certainly fail his Proelium," said Nicopolis. "Frankly, it has been like trying to teach a rock to swim. As for fieldwork, he's more likely to ruin a mission than assist you with one. I would leave him at home if I were you, when you're on call; he's quite good at cleaning. No sense endangering the humans in our charge with *him*."

No longer listening to Nicopolis, Basil watched as Griffin appeared at the end of the foyer and inched his way over to them, coming to a halt a few feet behind the other Mentor. Just out of reach, Basil thought to himself, noticing the cut lip and the guarded expression on Griffin's face. He waited until the Tiro glanced up at him, then he looked Griffin straight in the eye and smiled at him.

And for a fleeting moment, he thought he saw a faint smile back.

Chapter Two

Basil's Journal: Wednesday, June 9th

NICOPOLIS MAY HAVE A STERLING REPUTATION for training some of the best and the brightest Tiros, but I've never agreed with his harsh style. (In Griffin's case, I'm wondering just how brutal it was.) Beside the apparent lack of training, I think low self-esteem seems to be the lad's biggest issue.

Like most Terrae Angeli, he's keeping a journal. I'll encourage that as a form of therapy. I just won't call it therapy. He certainly doesn't need to feel that he's damaged goods. I have a strong suspicion Griffin has had enough of that already.

Griffin's Journal: Wednesday, June 9th

Basil wants me to keep writing in my journal (that's what he calls it—a *journal*) and that it'll help. Help with what? Chores?

His house is really different. It's small and old. Kind of messy, with stuff scattered all over it, especially books. All the other houses around here are old, too. The floors creak a lot! But I get my own bedroom. With a real bed. On the second floor. Even my own bathroom. He said I have to keep them clean. Think I can handle that, at least.

We ate lunch as soon as we got here. And I got to eat as much as I wanted.

Basil's Journal: Thursday, June 10th

I spent yesterday afternoon shopping for new clothes for Griffin and getting him settled in, then took him on a simple mission. He's quite behind other Tiros his age, so we're going to focus on basic skills. I flew solo and had him observe. I demonstrated to him how to cover his sudden appearance using a building or vegetation, and then perform the rescue with as little fanfare as possible.

Less is more.

I explained to him that humans in crisis mode tend not to pay attention to unusual occurrences. Which helps us fly under the proverbial radar screen and do our jobs more effectively. The young mother from today's mission just thought a nice man was in the right place at the right time to prevent her toddler from darting in front of a car.

I have always wondered how many humans might entertain the possibility that guardian angels really do exist.

In a way.

Using a different name, of course.

ᘓᘔ

Griffin crept downstairs with the dawn, his bare feet silent on the wooden steps. He winced when a tread creaked underfoot halfway down. Okay. Okay, he thought to himself. Skip the fourth one. Got it. He crossed the hallway and peeked around the door into Basil's study.

Breathing in the scent of leftover ashes in the fireplace, he slid inside the room and peered at a mound of files stacked to one side of the desk. Frowning, he read the label on the top one: *Griffin, Tiro.* 2008 *A.D.* He started to reach for it, his fingers hovering, then pulled his hand back. I don't want to know, he thought.

Tiptoeing through to the kitchen, Griffin made a beeline for the overhead cupboard next to the sink. He jumped at the sound of an abrupt wheeze as the nearby coffee maker started up, its timer emitting a shrill beep. "Fire!" he cursed, his heart hammering in his chest. "Stupid machine." Anxiously, he gazed at the ceiling overhead and waited for the sound of Basil's footsteps. After a few minutes of silence, he sighed in relief. Opening one cupboard door after another, he rummaged through each one, the percolating coffee filling the kitchen with an earthy scent.

Oh, gross, he thought, making a face as he spied a box of granola bars. Cardboard strips with raisins and cinnamon. Oh, well. At least they won't spoil. He grabbed a bar and peeled it open; munching, he stuffed the other bars into his back pocket. After glancing over his shoulder, he shoved the empty box toward the back of the shelf.

Leaning over the sink, he peered through the kitchen window at the backyard, then he slipped out the door and headed over to the garden bench in the corner, tucked under a blue spruce. He plopped down, digging his toes into the loose, moist soil under the evergreen. Feet half covered, he leaned against the wooden backrest and closed his eyes, unaware of the bars spilling out of his pocket and onto the ground beneath the bench. As he wiggled his toes, the nearby tree shivered from the roots upward, a few needles sprinkling down on his head. Oops, he thought. Better work on my Earth control. *He's* probably got some rule about that. That I just broke. Griffin sighed and rubbed a hand across his face. I wonder what's like *not* screwing up all the time.

"Why, good morning, Tiro."

Griffin's eyes flew open; he lurched to his feet and whirled around at the sound of Basil's voice. He watched warily as his Mentor, cradling a mug of coffee, smiled and sat down at the other end of the bench. Griffin noticed that his worn gray sweatshirt had ***Oxford*** emblazoned across the front of it.

"What are you doing out here so early?" Basil asked.

"Nothing, Mentor."

Basil cocked an eyebrow, then gestured to him to sit down again. "Well, since you're not otherwise occupied, you can listen to my quite popular 'new Tiro speech,'" he said.

Here it comes, thought Griffin, sinking down on the far edge of the bench. The lists of rules and chores. And punishments. He wiped his hands on his jeans, the new denim slick under his palms, and waited.

Basil drained his mug, then reached down and tucked it under the bench. He leaned back and gazed across the open field beyond their yard; on the western horizon, High Springs' famous peak was an indigo silhouette.

After a long minute, he lowered his head and turned, facing Griffin. "As you know, from this point on, you and I are a team. Mentor and Tiro. Angel and apprentice. And we both have our roles. It's important that I train you. And that you're prepared for your Proelium, eh?"

Griffin nodded, his face blank.

"But, it's equally important that you assist me on missions," Basil continued. "Because foremost—we are guardians. First responders for mortals, so to speak. Expect plenty of drills when we're on standby, but we'll do most of our training in the field."

He waited as Griffin shifted in his seat, looking down at his hands and picking at his ragged nails. "Lad, I've had twenty-two Tiros before you, so I can read you like the back of a cereal box. If you have a question, then spill it."

"What if I ..." began Griffin, then halted as his voice broke. He blushed, cleared his throat, and tried again. "What if I mess up? You know, on a mission? And a person gets hurt."

"The right question," said Basil, nodding with approval. "But you need not worry about that. It's *my* responsibility to make sure it never gets that far. There might be occasions I have to stop you or push you aside to aid a human. So when I say move, then for heaven's sake, *move*! Just don't take it personally."

Griffin nodded again.

"Not one for conversation, eh? Well, I don't blame you." Basil bent down, reaching for his cup, and stopped at the sight of several granola bars near Griffin's dirty feet. "How did these ...?" He scooped the snacks off the ground. "Did you bring these out here?"

"Yes, Mentor," he whispered.

"What are you doing with what appears to be the entire box? We're having breakfast soon and ..." His voice trailed away as he noticed Griffin's frightened expression. Nicopolis, he thought, struggling to keep his face composed. You monster. He took a deep breath. "Well, it doesn't matter. Here," he said, forcing a smile as he held them out. "Take these. I don't much care for this flavor. In fact, why don't you keep them in your room? In case you want a snack in the middle of the night." He waited, his arm outstretched.

Come on, lad. At least meet me halfway.

Griffin hesitated, then reached out and took the bars. "Thanks," he murmured.

"My pleasure," Basil said with studied casualness, as he stood up. Making a show of enjoying the sunrise, he watched Griffin out of the corner of his eye as the Tiro spat on his hands and leaned over, furtively wiping his dusty feet.

Basil looked away, then cleared his throat and said, in as natural a tone as he could manage, "Why don't you go rinse your feet at the faucet before you track in dirt." He nodded in the direction of the back door. "And roll your pant legs up first."

As Griffin went to wash, Basil lingered, his eyes fixed on heaven.

And made a silent promise.

Chapter Three

Griffin's Journal: Friday, June 11th

TODAY WE PRACTICED ELEMENT CONTROL. Which was good, because it's the only thing I can sort of do. Basil's got this big backyard, with an empty lot behind it, to train in. He said he hadn't worked with an Earth and Fire in a long time and was interested in what I could do. So I showed him how I heat the air, shake the ground, and some basic flame-handling. He seemed impressed. Except when my fireball got away from me and I lit up one of the pine trees. Luckily it was only a few branches. He just blasted it with water. Didn't get mad or scream at me or do anything ... else.

Basil's a Wind and Water, so his abilities are different from mine. He shot some gusts of wind and rain, and even made water ooze from the ground. He wants to try mixing our abilities in the next few days. Maybe try my earthquakes with his water-oozing-thing.

Don't know why I'm even thinking about it. It'll fail. Basil will get mad. I'll be blamed.

Basil's Journal: Monday, June 14th

I've discovered Griffin was hoarding food. More than just granola bars. I made it clear to him that this was his home now. And that he was welcome to anything and everything. Anytime.

He's quite anxious. Flinches whenever I come too near, and is practically OCD about cleaning. Heaven help him if this is his true nature.

On a brighter note: Griffin and I combined his earth-shaking ability with my pooling technique. Brilliant! The back corner of our yard is now a massive quagmire. I'm leaving it there. It could come in handy.

I think we'll try some Might use in the next day or so.

ꙮ

"Right. Try blocking this one," said Basil, flinging a small pebble. He winced when it bounced off Griffin's forehead. "Oops! My apologies, Tiro." He scanned the vacant field beyond the high stone wall for any spectators. "Thank heaven our backyard's secluded—all we need is a meddlesome neighbor catching me chucking rocks at you, eh?"

His eyes watering, Griffin nodded and rubbed his brow. Come on, he thought to himself. Block it! Before he gets mad. He braced his feet as Basil tossed another stone.

It skipped off his skull again with a dull thunk. He staggered backwards, then tripped, landing on his bottom with a grunt. "Oh, Fire!" he cursed under his breath, rubbing his head. He flinched when a shadow fell across him.

Basil knelt beside him. "It's an acceptable strategy to duck, lad."

Resisting the urge to lean away, Griffin tucked his arm tight against his body, his eyes fixed on the ground. He waited until the Mentor rose, then got to his feet and took a step back nervously; he looked up surprised when Basil chuckled.

"Well, I'll say this about you. You've a hard head. Although it sounded suspiciously hollow." He raised an eyebrow at Griffin's solemn expression. "You have permission to laugh at my jokes."

"Yes, sir."

Basil sighed. Looking around the yard, he thought for a minute, then walked over and picked up one of the many cardboard boxes scattered about. Stacking it on top of a larger one, he stepped to one side.

"Let's try something different," said Basil. "Now, concentrate on those boxes. All I want you to do is push the top box over. Don't try to *move* it, just *push* it. Use any technique you've got.

"Yes, sir." Taking a deep breath, Griffin flung his hand out, palm forward, at the boxes.

Nothing happened.

"Try again," Basil said, nodding toward the stack. "And this time, slow down and use a smaller amount. You'll have more control that way. We're just moving some boxes, not the Rocky Mountains. Remember the sequence: first, gather the Might within you; next, gain control of it; then finally, release it."

Griffin nodded. He squeezed his eyes shut and clenched his jaw, holding his breath as he waited for the power to flow into him. To fill the hollow space inside. How can I control it when I don't even know what it's supposed to feel like? After a few moments, he opened his eyes in defeat.

"Sorry," he whispered.

'Don't be. We'll just keep practicing. Every Tiro masters Might at their own speed," explained Basil. "You'll get there eventually. And you will find it a handy tool on missions." He smiled. "However, your control of both Earth and Fire is quite advanced for a Tiro your age."

"It ... it is?"

Basil laughed at Griffin's sudden astonishment. "I'll assume Nicopolis didn't teach you those techniques."

"Um ... no, sir. I figured it out on my own."

"Most of my other Earth and Fire Tiros were older and more experienced before they could do what you did the other day with that fireball. So let's practice that for a while." Basil pointed to the stacked boxes. "Throw a fireball at the top box."

Griffin frowned in confusion. He looked over at the boxes, and then back at his Mentor. "I don't understand."

"Throw a fireball at the top box," Basil repeated. "Just like you did the other day. Except the box, not the tree, please." He crossed his arms over his broad chest and waited.

"Okay," said Griffin reluctantly. He turned and drew his arm back, his lips pressed into a thin line as he concentrated. The air shimmered around him; his hair stood on end and waved from the heat.

Flames ignited in his hand with a dull whoosh. Curling his fingers around them, he formed them into a ball, then took a deep breath and pitched.

The fireball whizzed across the yard, engulfing the box and sending it soaring toward the fence with a roar. It landed under the lilac bush; the purple blossoms sagged like melted crayons.

"Good heavens!" Basil hurriedly pointed a finger, spraying the box and leaving a charred, but soggy, lump of cardboard on the lawn. He turned back, beaming at Griffin. "Well? What are you waiting for?" he shouted happily. "Launch another one!"

Basil hit the ground just in time. A second box jetted past his head as it raced toward the quagmire in the corner, the heat from it crinkling the hairs on his arms and the back of his neck. Rolling over, he gestured overhead. A miniature storm cloud formed above the house, then sped to hover directly over the puddle and began raining on it.

Leaping to his feet, Basil brushed grass from his tee shirt. "Brilliant! Now keep going, lad! I want every box in this yard flaming like a meteor into that puddle!"

Squaring his shoulders, Griffin shook out his hands and flexed his fingers, his heart thumping with anticipation. Okay, *this* I can do, he thought.

As he blasted box after box, he felt a grin spreading across his face. With each fireball, he grew stronger, the energy from the Element surging through his body. "Watch this one, Basil!" he shouted without thinking. Blinking the sweat out of his eyes, he sucked in a deep breath and launched the final box, emptying the puddle and sending scalding water into the air like a geyser. "Yes!" he cried, punching his fist into the air. His chest heaving, he pushed his damp hair off his forehead, and turned to Basil, who was standing a few yards away.

A smile on his rugged face, the Mentor inclined his head to his Tiro, as if bowing to an equal. "Now tell me that wasn't fun?"

Griffin sneezed. Then laughed.

Chapter Four

Basil's Journal: Wednesday, July 7th

I'VE WORKED WITH MY NEW TIRO for several weeks now. I occasionally catch glimmers of a different Griffin. Maybe the real Griffin. One that is a bit more relaxed. A little more capable. Even a lad with a sense of humor. I wouldn't mind seeing more of those Griffins.

For the record, he has allergies. Fire makes him sneeze.

Griffin's Journal: Friday, July 16th

For some reason, Basil changed our entire cover story. I like this new one better. He told me to practice descriptive writing once in a while instead of teen angst (he does this funny thing with his face that means he's kidding around), so my assignment is to describe both our cover story and us.

He wants to read them when I'm done. He said it was to check how well I focused on details. Great. Now I have homework!

Mentor Basil: about 40 earth years old. He has an English accent. Really tall (six feet, four inches, he told me) and in pretty good shape. Short white hair (not gray, but white like clouds) and really blue eyes and a reddish complexion (I think the word is *ruddy)*. Usually wears jeans and a white shirt. Sometimes a sports coat. I looked up the meaning of his name. In Greek, it means *noble* or *kingly*. It fits him.

Tiro Griffin: about 13 earth years, average height (five feet, eight inches) and average build. I have dark brown hair (with a little red in it) and brown eyes, and I tan easily. I usually wear a tee shirt and jeans. Basil said I was a 'true reflection of my Elements.' Whatever that means.

Cover Story: We're supposed to be father and son. Our last name is Raine. We live in High Springs. It's the second largest city in Colorado. My mother is dead. Father is retired British Intelligence. Still does consulting work. I'm thirteen and home-schooled.

Hope that's what you wanted, Basil.

Basil's Journal: Monday, July 19th

Amusing—Griffin's description of the two of us. (I sensed he had misgivings about my British Intelligence background story—detected a bit of an eye-roll from him. I think it shows a certain flair myself.) However, I was impressed by some of his vocabulary words, and especially his research. (Note to self: Griffin to research *Griffin*)

Griffin's Journal: Tuesday, July 20th

Griffin – Welsh for *strong in faith.*

I don't think it fits me at all. Besides, it's a stupid name.

Basil's Journal: Wednesday, July 28th

I haven't had a moment to even floss my teeth, much less update this journal! We've had back-to-back missions for several days running, but nothing tricky. Just good solid field training for Griffin.

Basil's Journal: Sunday, August 1st

Glory!

Griffin had his first successful solo mission this morning.

The Rock Garden State Park. Popular rock climbing area. Late morning.

All I can say is that it was a good thing I hid behind those trees. It certainly would have ruined it for Griffin to see me helpless with laughter. He did everything right; just needs to work on hand placement.

He tried to be nonchalant about today's accomplishment. Still keeping that protective wall up around himself. Yet today he was practically vibrating with joy over his victory.

I know something about Griffin he doesn't know himself yet, but will soon realize: safeguarding human beings means everything to him.

It is why he was created.

Griffin's Journal: Sunday, August 1st

I bagged one this morning! A solo mission, too. Well, Basil waited behind some trees. Just in case. The woman was grateful, but her husband? Not so much. I didn't mean to grab her butt; it was just the safest way to shove her back up the rock face as she started to slip.

Basil seemed pretty happy. He said my timing was perfect, but I needed to think about the position of my hands or something like that.

Maybe I'm not so stupid. Maybe I can do this.

Chapter Five

"Are we training here?" asked Griffin, hopping out of the Saab and looking around the small parking lot, pine trees and scrub oak crowding it along three sides. "Won't people still see us?"

Basil locked the car door and nodded toward a dirt path winding away into the woods; a sign adorned with a multicolored map declared the beginning of the wilderness area. "Actually, I'm taking you to a meadow that is secluded enough for our purpose. With the rumbling and quaking you're going to produce, it's best we practice on the outskirts of town." He glanced up with a smile at the afternoon sky, a perfect summer blue, then started toward to the trailhead.

"Um ... can I?" Griffin nodded toward a nearby brick structure, an apologetic smile on his face.

"I thought you went before we left?"

"I did, b-but I had that soda and the rest of yours, so...."

Basil rolled his eyes. "Go on, then." He flapped a hand at the restroom.

After a minute, Griffin sauntered out. He broke into a jog as he hurried after Basil, already hiking up the path flanked by fragrant pine and spruce. Catching up, he marched alongside, taking two steps for every one of his Mentor's. As the trail led deeper into the foothills, they began climbing, heading due west.

"Basil?"

"Fin."

"Aren't we on call right now?"

"That we are, lad, but Command can contact us here as easily as at home. And since you're becoming more adept at appearing and disappearing, we've a bit more flexibility." After several more yards, he veered to the north. "Right. Here we go," he said, plunging off the well-used path and following a faint passage through the dense scrub. For fifteen minutes, they forced a way through the vegetation until they emerged into a small clearing.

"What are those?" Griffin pointed at grassy mounds of earth scattered across the area. He followed Basil to the center of the space.

"Oh, leftovers from previous sessions." Basil glanced around. "In fact, we might as well use them."

"Use them for what?"

"Why, for practice! Now, tell me, Tiro," he said in his best instructor voice, "what can you do with Earth?"

Griffin grinned. "Hit it or split it." He bounced lightly on the balls of his feet.

Basil chuckled at his eagerness. "Can't wait to show off, eh? Well, then you best demonstrate what you can do." He pointed over Griffin's shoulder. "I want you to open a crevasse under that mound. The one near the large pine." He raised a finger in warning. "But make sure you avoid the tree. Control is just as important as power."

"Yes, sir!" Griffin spun around, dropped to one knee, and punched his fist into the ground, wincing from the blow. With a deep groan, the ground cracked open, the split ripping along toward the dirt pile, the tall grass on either side folding over with a sigh. As the ravine approached, the mound sagged, then crumbled into the trench and disappeared. Griffin jumped to his feet. Massaging his knuckles, he looked expectantly at his Mentor. His smile of triumph faded as he saw Basil's expression. "What's the matter—" he started to ask, and then hunched his shoulders at the sound of snapping and crashing behind him. He glanced around and stared in dismay at the sight of the pine settling lengthwise across the ravine, its roots torn up, its broken branches scattering across the ground. "Sorry," he muttered, then sighed in relief at Basil's chuckle.

"Well, you're not the first Tiro to fell a tree like that. But it appears you need to work on—" He froze as a shaft of Light stabbed the clearing, illuminating the area with a white radiance. As the voice spoke from within it, Basil listened intently, motioning for Griffin to take a stand next to him. "Right. We're on our way," he responded as the beam faded, then glanced down. "We must hurry, lad."

Griffin gave a nod. Side by side, they shot forward, running a few strides before leaping into the air.

They vanished in a gust of wind.

ཀ୦ଔ

Griffin crashed to his knees from the force of his landing. Panting, he jumped to his feet, spun around, and began scrambling up the steep slope toward Basil, his hands and toes digging in as he slipped on the loose gravel and dirt. "Oh, Fire!" he gasped as he looked past his Mentor.

A Jeep skidded off the shoulder of the dirt road above him and rolled over the embankment, picking up speed as it slid on its side toward them. The screech of metal battering against rocks and fallen trees tore the afternoon air apart as dirt billowed up around it.

"Griffin! Get out of the way!" Basil shouted over the noise, then vanished; a flash of white light burst from the Jeep's backseat.

Before Griffin could move, the vehicle shot past him; gravel stung his face as it missed him by inches. His mouth and eyes filled with dust, he dropped to his knees and slammed both fists into the ground. With a low groan, an earthen embankment erupted directly in the path of the Jeep; it grew larger, forming a dirt ramp. The wreck plowed up the incline, slowed, then tipped upright, coming to a shuddering halt on its flat tires.

"Basil!" Leaping to his feet, Griffin tore down the slope and skidded to a stop beside the wreckage. The ground was littered by shattered glass and twisted metal. "Basil," he screamed again as he spotted his Mentor curled around a yellow bundle in the back seat. He grabbed the smashed handle and jerked as hard as he could; cursing when the door refused to budge.

"Griffin! Easy, lad," called a muffled voice from inside the vehicle.

"Basil! A-are you okay?" Griffin squinted through the spider-webbed glass. Relief flooded through him at the sight of his Mentor's calm face. As he watched, Basil uncurled, revealing a baby girl clasped against his chest. The remnants of a child seat lay next to him.

"I'm fine, as is this little one here. But I'm afraid her parents were not so fortunate."

Griffin closed his eyes for a moment. My fault, he thought. I was too late with that ramp. He swallowed the lump in his throat. "What do I do now?" he asked.

"Stand back and I'll get this open."

After Griffin stepped away, Basil pressed his free hand against the door and pushed. With an ear-piercing squeal, it ripped free of its hinges and crashed to the ground. He crawled out, the child still cradled in one arm; with his other hand, he pulled his cell phone out of his pocket and flipped it open.

As Basil began dialing, Griffin stared into the baby's face. The baby gazed back, her eyes full of trust.

"Dogs and small children, eh?" remarked Basil.

"What's that mean?" Griffin asked.

"Oh, it's an old wives' tale. Dogs and children, because of their innocent natures, can recognize what we truly are."

As Basil spoke into the phone, Griffin held out a finger to the baby, smiling weakly when she grasped it with a tenacious hold. "I'm sorry," he whispered to her. "I should have been faster. Then your mom and dad would still be alive." He looked away and blinked, his eyes stinging from sudden tears.

Must be the gasoline fumes, he lied to himself.

Griffin's Journal: Saturday, August 21st

Basil told me to keep a record of all of my missions. I really don't want to. Not all of them.

Basil's Journal: Saturday, August 21st

I should prepare dinner. Which neither of us will eat, of course. Still, we need to keep up our strength. We're on call for another five hours.

Griffin's upstairs— he is quite distraught. How do I explain that we can't save them all? We're not omnipotent. Not us.

Sometimes, as a terrestrial angel, I do envy celestial angels. It must be comforting never to fail a task.

ꙮ

Basil's eyes flew open. He raised his head off his pillow, frowning as he listened. At the second cry, he rolled out of bed. I *knew* today's tragedy would bring on another bloody nightmare! he fumed. Wrenching his door open, he grabbed a robe, flinging it on over his tee shirt and pajama pants as he hurried down the hallway, his feet thudding on the wooden floor. He eased inside Griffin's bedroom, finding his Tiro pressed against the headboard, panting, arms spread wide on either side as if braced for a fall. Basil stayed near the open doorway. "Fin. It's me. May I come in?" he said in a low voice.

Griffin glanced up, and then nodded. His face gleamed with sweat in the dim light of the street lamp outside his window.

Basil ambled over and perched on the side of the bed. "Bad dream?"

Griffin nodded again and then cleared his throat. "Kind of," he rasped. "I can't remember now. Just trying to get away, but..." His voice trailed off.

"But unable to?" Basil finished his sentence for him.

"Yeah." He let out a shaky breath and wiped his forehead, grimacing at the feel of sweat-soaked hair. "Sorry I'm such a wimp." He laughed softly, embarrassed, his brown eyes dark in his pale face as he stared into the shadows.

"You certainly are not. And besides, everyone has nightmares, lad."

"Even you?"

"Even I."

"About what?"

"Running out of coffee."

Griffin snorted.

"Right," said Basil, smiling back. "Now, I believe there's a pie in our kitchen that needs to be sampled. Right now. And I, for one, hate to binge by myself." He jumped up and flipped the heavy quilt over Griffin's head, adding a spare pillow for good measure.

"Hey! What the ...?" Griffin complained, his voice muffled.

"Last one downstairs has clean-up duty," Basil announced and sprinted out of the room. Hearing Griffin kick free of the covers and pound after him, he grinned, glancing over his shoulder.

"No, Tiro!" He skidded to a stop and whirled around. "No flying—" he began, then groaned as Griffin cannonballed over the banister and vanished in mid air "—inside the house." He winced at the sound of a heavy thud in the hallway below. Hurrying down the stairs, he shook his head at the sight of Griffin sprawled on his side, rubbing his tailbone.

"Ow! Right on my butt!"

"Still having trouble with short flights, eh?" he said as he took Griffin's arm and hauled him upright.

Griffin grimaced. "It's not the flights, it's the landings." Limping slightly, he led the way to the kitchen.

Basil chuckled as he followed. "But since technically, you did arrive first, I believe *I* have cleaning duty."

"Spot on," said the Tiro in his best English accent.

Basil smiled to himself.

Chapter Six

Basil's Journal: Tuesday, August 24th

WE'VE HAD FOURTEEN MISSIONS IN A ROW over the last few days. I'm so weary that I'm typing this with one hand. Heavens, one *finger*! I need the other hand to prop up my head.

Fourteen missions. Eleven victories. Eight due to our solid teamwork. It's unbelievable how quickly Griffin is improving. Field training is the best thing in the world for him.

Griffin's Journal: Wednesday, August 25th

Slept nine hours, but I still feel wasted. Basil crashed in the study on the sofa. The dude snores! His computer was on. I guess he was working on his journal when he zonked out. For just a moment, I wanted to look at it. But then I thought how I'd feel if he looked at mine. So I didn't.

I made coffee for him, instead. I had it ready when he woke up.

ॐ

"I'll get it," called Basil as the doorbell rang. He hurried down the hall, the mid-morning sun pouring in the open door. Peering through the screen, he beamed with delight. "Lena! How are you? Come in, please!" He held it open for the silver-haired woman and bent to kiss her wrinkled cheek.

"Hello, Basil," said Lena Weiss, smiling as she patted his arm. "I hope you don't mind me stopping by unannounced. I took the chance that you might be home to drop off the documents." She hefted a briefcase. "And, of course, to meet Griffin. It's already been two months and I haven't yet laid eyes on the boy! Is this a good time or are you two on call?"

"No, your timing is excellent. We're off rotation this morning, thank heaven, and I've just brewed fresh coffee. Make yourself at home." Basil gestured, then headed to the kitchen, pausing at the foot of the stairs. "Griffin! Come down to the study, please. There's someone I want you to meet!"

As Basil continued toward the kitchen, Griffin padded barefoot down the stairs and along the hall toward their study. He froze in the doorway at the sight of Lena opening a briefcase resting on the coffee table. As he watched, she pulled out a thick file and a small square box, then looked up.

"Good morning! You must be Griffin." He nodded as she continued, "I'm Lena Weiss. An old friend of Basil's and your liaison with the Foundation. I was hoping we'd meet today."

He glanced over his shoulder, and then eased into the room. "Um ... hi." Foundation, he thought to himself. What's a Foundation? Unsure what to do, he stood there until Basil appeared behind him, a tray balanced in his hands.

"Fin, you're blocking the door. Go take a seat." Griffin headed over to a chair next to the fireplace as Basil set the tray on his cluttered desk. He handed a cup and saucer to Lena. "Cream, no sugar, right? And did you two meet?"

"We did. Oh, thank you," she said as she took the cup and placed it on the side table. Picking up the file in front of her, she flipped it open and began laying out several documents. "I think I have everything you asked for. Let's see—birth certificate, social security number and card, and a passport. I chose October first for his birthday. That'll make him fourteen in a few months." She smiled apologetically at Griffin. "You must wait for the driver's license a bit longer, yes?"

"Nationality?" Basil gathered up the papers and rifled through them as he walked around his desk and took his seat.

"I managed a dual citizenship—British and American. I thought that would be an appropriate match for your cover story. Oh, and I opened an account for him at your bank. Just in case." Lena settled back and picked up her cup. As she took a sip from it, she noticed Griffin's confused expression.

"Do you have any questions I can answer?" she asked. I'm glad Basil filled me in, she thought. Poor liebling.

At Basil's prompting, Griffin nodded. "What's a lass ... less yon ...?" he asked, stammering over the unfamiliar word. He peered at the pile on the desk. "Is that stuff about me?"

"The word is *liaison*, and Miss Weiss is ours. With the Foundation," said Basil. "Do you know what I'm talking about, lad? Not a clue, eh?"

Leaning back in his chair, he tapped the documents with his finger.

"The Foundation is an organization of humans who help Terrae Angeli with the logistics of daily life. Each Terrae Angelus, or in our case, each team, has a person who helps us with things like documents, money, housing, transportation, and so on. We are more effective in our roles as guardian angels if we fit in with human society. The more seamless the fit, the more good we can do. The North American Foundation has been around since the mid-sixteen-hundreds. I believe the oldest branch is in Virginia."

"Humans know about us?"

"Very few. Lena and I met years ago in East Berlin when she was a child. Her family was fleeing to America and Lena became separated. To make a short story shorter—I found her, smuggled her out of East Germany and into the United States, and reunited her with her family."

"I never forgot the tall *man* who saved me." Lena picked up the story. "And his remarkable tale of the Terrae Angeli. I've always felt ... honored ... that he revealed his true nature to me. Later, I decided to become part of the Foundation. Your Mentor and I have worked together for years now and I've known a few of his other Tiros." She smiled with delight. "And spoiled them whenever I could. Here, Griffin, this is for you." Lena handed him a small package.

He took it and glanced at Basil. His Mentor nodded. His eyes wide with curiosity, Griffin popped the lid open and pulled out an expensive sports watch and a folded set of directions. "Oh, awesome!" He examined it, tilting the face back and forth. "Thank you, Miss Weiss."

"You can put it on, Fin. That's the whole point of a wrist watch," said Basil. Griffin's smile lit up the room as he strapped it to his arm.

"Let me see," said Basil. Griffin leaned over, his hand stuck out proudly. "That has every bell and whistle, to be sure." Picking up the directions, he handed them to Griffin. "Take these up to your room now so you won't lose them. Shoo."

Griffin jumped up. "Uh...thank you again," he said as he left. Halfway to the stairs, he stopped and whirled around. I forgot the box. I think I want to keep that, too. As he took a step back, he froze at the mention of his name. Moving stealthily on bare toes, he pressed himself against the wall near the door.

"So, what do you think of Griffin?" he heard Basil ask.

"It's difficult to tell," Lena said. "He's quite reserved, but maybe that's meeting me for the first time, yes? How are missions and training going?"

"That's a complicated question. In some areas, he's terribly behind. In particular, his use of Might."

Griffin winced.

"However, his Element control is incredible, especially fire. So I'm teaching him to compensate. Use skills he excels at to overcome skills he lacks. Our missions have been more and more successful, which boosts his self-confidence. Thank heaven we have a few years until his Proelium."

At the mention of the trial, Griffin's stomach clenched. Okay, don't think about it! he ordered himself. It's still a long ways away. And maybe I'll get better at stuff before then. He leaned closer as Lena cleared her throat.

"Basil, tell me something. Do *you* agree with this testing method? The Proelium?"

"No, of course not. It's brutal and archaic. And we abandon our young ones when they fail and need us the most."

"So why—" began Lena.

"Because we are not raising children, Lena," interrupted Basil. "We are training soldiers."

"It's cruel."

"Perhaps. Perhaps not. If they cannot succeed as angels, isn't it better they know by sixteen so they can begin a new life as a human?" Basil argued, and then snorted ruefully. "I guess I'd feel differently if it were ever one of my Tiros who failed."

Griffin blinked in astonishment. He sounds like he thinks I'm actually going to pass!

"Oh, dear," Lena sighed, closing her briefcase with a snap. "I'd better leave. I've got a meeting in forty-five minutes and the Interstate is still a mess from construction."

Oh, crap! thought Griffin. Darting across the hall, he dashed around the archway and tucked himself inside the living room. His pulse pounding in his ears, he struggled to hear Basil and Lena talking as they lingered by the front screen.

"Thank you again. For everything," said Basil. "Griffin appreciated that watch. He so rarely smiles; it was a gift for *me* to actually see one!"

"Why, then next time, I'll bring him a pony," she said. After a moment, the screen slapped shut.

Griffin bit his lip to keep from laughing. He crept over and peeked around the corner of the doorway. Spotting Basil through the screen, he took a deep breath and pasted a smile on his face, then slipped out and joined him on the porch. "I ... uh ... just wanted to say good-bye," he said, the lie nipping at him.

They both waved as Lena idled in the street. She rolled down her window and called to them.

"*Auf Wiedersehen,* you two! Griffin, take good care of your Mentor!"

"That's a *tall* order, Miss Weiss," he yelled back, looking up at Basil in mock exaggeration.

Basil's Journal: Thursday, August 26th

I thought Lena was going to drive onto the curb, she was laughing so hard. It was a terribly lame joke, but still ....

Griffin's Journal: Thursday, August 26th

Miss Weiss's pretty cool—she brought some papers and stuff Basil said I needed and even a new watch. And I learned about the Foundation.

But I wished I hadn't eavesdropped.

Chapter Seven

Basil's Journal: Friday, September 17th

SPEAK OF THE DEVIL: guess who showed up today while I was out?

ᘐᘓ

"Stupid bloody..." said Griffin under his breath as the board toppled over again, then he laughed. "I'm starting to sound like Basil." He stalked over, the early autumn leaves crunching underfoot, and heaved the large wooden target back upright. Propping it securely with a rock, he hurried to the other side of the yard and turned around, pushing at the sleeves of his hoodie. Extending his right hand, the first two fingers pointing like spears, Griffin blasted one pea-size fireball after another at the panel, their high-pitched whine barely audible. Wisps of smoke trickled out of each tiny hole.

"And the spectators go wild!" he crowed, eyeing the scorch marks in and around the center of the bull's-eye. He sneezed and wiped his nose with the palm of his hand. This is so slick, he thought. I can't wait to show Basil. How many times a month does he get his hair cut, anyway?

He started forward, then halted, wide-eyed as the target began vibrating. With a gasp, he ducked, crouching as it leaped up and whirled past his head, crashing against the back wall and splintering into pieces. "What the ...?" He frowned at the pile of wood, and then froze, the hairs on the back of his neck standing up. Holding his breath, he turned around.

Nicopolis stood behind him.

Griffin backed up and tripped, tumbling to the ground. Rolling over, he scuttled sideways on his hands and feet as he tried to get up, get away.

"Why, Tiro! Aren't you pleased to see me?" Nicopolis sneered as he stepped closer and reached down, snagging the front of Griffin's sweat top in his fist. "Stand when a Mentor is speaking to you." He hauled him to his feet. "Or have you forgotten your manners?" Gripping tightly with one hand, he reached into his pocket with the other and yanked out a folded sheet of parchment. "Do you know what this is?" he asked. He snapped it open and waved it in Griffin's face.

Griffin stared, his heart hammering against his ribs while a voice screamed in his head. *Run! Or fight back! But don't just take it!*

"It's a complaint lodged with Flight Command concerning my training methods." He pulled Griffin closer, until their noses were almost touching. "You little weasel. You thought you might get back at me, did you?" he hissed, his breath stale. "A permanent warning on my record? Perhaps get me stripped of my rank as a Senior Mentor?" He shoved him away. Eyes blazing, he crumpled the paper in his fist and tossed it aside. "Fortunately I was able to smooth it over with Command. Somewhat."

"I ... I didn't ..." Griffin began, shaking his head in confusion.

"No. I did." They both turned at the voice by the back door.

Basil marched across the yard, his face impassive. Reaching Griffin's side, he kept his eyes locked on Nicopolis. "*I* spoke with Flight Command about you, not Griffin."

Nicopolis smirked. "I see. Still jealous of my status, old friend?"

"Riiight," drawled Basil. "Because my ultimate goal in life is to be a tyrant and a bully. Just like you, *old friend*." He stepped closer to Nicopolis. "I suggest you leave. Now."

"Or what? Another Might to Might brawl? Like when we were Tiros?"

Basil shrugged. "As you wish," he said softly, his blue eyes darkening. He adjusted his stance and straightened to his full height.

Without thinking, Griffin stepped closer on shaky legs, taking a defensive posture to one side of Basil. He cupped his hands, igniting a fire ball in each one and waited.

Nicopolis' mouth twisted. His eyes flicked once toward Griffin, then back to Basil. With a snarl, he spun around and disappeared in a blast of wind, the garden gate slamming against the side of the house.

Letting out a breath, Basil stared at the empty spot in front of him for a moment. "Well, that was a less than cordial exchange," he said and turned around. "And what are those for?"

Griffin glanced down at the smoking fireballs. "Just in case," he whispered, then clenched his hands into fists and extinguished the flames. As Basil started toward him, Griffin's legs gave out. Falling to his knees, he bent forward, pressing his damp forehead against the cool lawn. He swallowed, then swallowed again, fighting the fear burning his throat.

"Fin?" Basil crouched next to him.

"I'm okay." He cleared his throat. "Just something I ate." He sat up, dusting dried grass off his bangs, and then spat to one side.

"Of course it was." Basil stood up, took his elbow and helped him to his feet. Guiding him toward the house, he looked at him out of the corner of his eye. "So. Would you have really thrown them? At Nicopolis?"

"I ... I don't know." Maybe, he thought to himself. I hope so.

"Well, I'm proud of your willingness to defend yourself. Against a Mentor, no less. Against *him*, no less." Basil stepped aside, waving the Tiro through the back door.

Griffin paused and looked up. "It wasn't me I was defending."

Griffin's Journal: Saturday, September 18th

Basil wants me to write about yesterday. I really don't want to, but he asked me to try. Okay. Fine.

Nicopolis came by. A bunch of stuff happened. He left. Then we went inside.

Basil's Journal: Sunday, September 19th

I'll give him a few days, but I think it's time we talked.

Basil's Journal: Wednesday, September 22nd

One-thirty in the morning. We've just finished up. Griffin told me everything about his years with Nicopolis. Most of it, I had already guessed; still, it was almost unbearable to hear the details from Fin. About the lack of training and impossible expectations. The verbal attacks. The beatings. Nicopolis' volatile temper. The lack of food, the lack of sleep. He kept asking me if it was his fault. Maybe if he hadn't been so clumsy or stupid or lazy, then Nicopolis would have liked him. Or at least not hated him.

I can hardly type—my hands are trembling so much.

Griffin's curled up on the sofa in the study, sound asleep under the old plaid blanket. He didn't even wake when I pulled his shoes off.

The shakes hit him quite hard about an hour ago. Warm milk with nutmeg helped. I had a shot of something a little stronger.

In the midst of this dark night, Griffin made two important decisions: His past will be a part of him, but will not define him. And we are now friends. As well as Mentor and Tiro.

ꕥ

Basil hit the save button and rubbed his tired eyes. Leaning back in his desk chair, he swiveled around and gazed at Griffin for a minute, his fingers drumming on the desk. He stood up, stretching his back, and then walked over to the bookshelf and pulled out a tome, its leather cover dry with age. Turning the pages in a delicate rustle, he searched intently until he found the correct section. Holding it open in one hand, he walked over and knelt by the sofa. "Fin," he said softly.

Griffin blinked, squinting as he looked up. "Are we on call?" he asked, his voice rough from sleep.

"No. But I need you awake for this." He waited as the young angel shoved the blanket to one side and sat up, bleary-eyed, his hair squashed flat on one side.

Basil laid his free hand on Griffin's head, his voice resolute as he read aloud the ancient blessing, armoring his Tiro against the evils of the world. Both worlds. After he finished, he shrugged at Griffin's unspoken question. "Just in case."

Chapter Eight

GRIFFIN CHEWED HIS THUMBNAIL as he stared across Command's meeting room and out the bank of windows lining the far wall; the October sky was a flawless blue. Fire, I don't want be here, he thought. They have that report. Why do they have to talk with me about it? With *him* here? He began to gnaw the other thumbnail.

"That's enough," said Basil, with a poke of his elbow. "I thought we had broken you of that habit." He frowned as he checked his watch. "I wonder what's delaying them?" They both looked over when the double doors at the end of the room opened.

Nicopolis strolled in, the doors closing with a click behind him.

Griffin's heart slammed against his ribs. He watched Nicopolis walk around to the far side, unbuttoning his suit coat as he took a seat.

"Well, well," Nicopolis said with a sneer as he settled back. "If it isn't Batman and Robin."

"Batman and Robin, eh?" said Basil. "So that would make you the Penguin?" His smile never reached his eyes. Griffin snickered in spite of his dread. He raised his chin as Nicopolis glared at him.

At that moment, the massive doors swung open again. A graceful figure in a turquoise sari walked in with a file tucked under her arm; her long, blue-black hair flowed down her back like a veil. "Good afternoon, all," she said briskly as she paused at the head of the table. Her face softened as she glanced at Basil who had risen. To Griffin's surprise, she put down her folder and held out her slender hands. Basil clasped them in both of his.

"Mayla," he said warmly. "It's been far too long, my friend."

"At least, you didn't call me *old* friend," she replied, her lips curving into a smile.

"Certainly not! I learned *that* lesson," Basil said, his eyes twinkling, "as a young and rather foolish Tiro."

They both laughed and stood gazing at each other for a long minute until Nicopolis cleared his throat.

"Well, well," he said. "I appear to be at a disadvantage already. I had forgotten how *close* you and Basil were when we were Tiros."

"Close?" whispered Griffin, looking up wide-eyed at his Mentor.

"Drop it, Tiro," Basil muttered back out of the side of his mouth.

Mayla arched a delicate eyebrow as she let go of Basil's hands and looked at Nicopolis. "Disadvantage? In what way?" She sat down as Basil resumed his seat.

"Isn't it obvious?" he replied.

She rolled her eyes. "Ah, Nicopolis. Only *you* would immediately presume that I am unable or unwilling to be neutral in this situation." Shaking her head, she added, "some things never change—you always assume the worst in others." Ignoring his protests, she folded her hands in a jingle of bracelets, then leaned forward, and looked at Griffin.

"Tiro Griffin," she began in a business-like manner. "I am Guardian Mayla. I am here to investigate the accusations made against Mentor Nicopolis. This is not a trial, but simply a meeting between all the parties involved to determine the truth. Do you understand?"

Griffin nodded. Under the table, he pressed his sweaty palms against his knees.

"Then let us proceed," she said, pulling the first sheet of paper out of the folder.

ꙮ

"He's lying. About everything," Nicopolis hissed, his face livid as he glared across the table at Basil. "Manufacturing stories to get sympathy from you and leniency from Command!"

"Really?" Basil narrowed his eyes. "And why would he do that?"

"To cover up his incompetence, of course," said Nicopolis. "He knew his apprenticeship was doomed so he shifted the blame from himself to me. And my training methods."

As Basil began to speak, Mayla interrupted him. "I've heard enough during this last hour." She glanced at Nicopolis, then Basil. "From *both* of you." After scribbling some notes in the file, the scratching of her pen harsh in the silent room, she looked up at Griffin. "Well, Tiro. Do you have anything you wish to add?"

"I...I told the truth," he said, trying to keep his voice steady. He balled his hands into fists under the table as he glared at Nicopolis. "And I know what you think, but you're wrong. About me."

Mayla pursed her lips as she toyed with her pen. "We Terrae Angeli walk a fine line in the training of our apprentices," she said. "Push them too hard and it looks like abuse. Coddle them too much and they go into the field unprepared, and possibly are injured or killed on missions." She sighed and reached over, closing the file. "Well, I see no *solid* proof of mistreatment or neglect on the part of Mentor Nicopolis," she began, then lifted her hand, forestalling any outburst from Basil or gloating from Nicopolis.

"However, Nicopolis, you should know that Command will be entering this incident in your permanent file. It may or may not have an impact in any future advancement you seek." She rose, the other three following suit. "Basil, it was good to see you. And I hope we meet again soon. Under more pleasant circumstances." She started to say something else, then stopped. "This meeting is adjourned." After picking up her papers, she nodded and left, leaving the doors open behind her.

For a moment, none of them moved.

Then Basil sighed. "Less than I had hoped," he said. Ignoring the other Mentor, he led the way toward the exit, Griffin a few steps behind. They both halted and turned when Nicopolis laughed softly.

"Unbelievable!" He walked around the table, his pale eyes boring into Griffin's as he approached him. "You've managed to ruin my career, after all. Simply by being your worthless self."

Griffin stared back, grateful for Basil's presence. "It wasn't my fault –"

"Oh, but it was." Nicopolis stepped closer. "And this is not over. Not at all."

"A threat?" Basil asked, a warning tone in his voice.

"A promise," said Nicopolis. Without another word, he pushed past them and left. They looked at each other, unease mirrored in their eyes. Then suddenly Griffin laughed.

Basil raised an eyebrow. "I fail to see the humor, Tiro."

"Batman and Robin," he said with a grin. "You got to admit, that was pretty good. For *him*." Falling into step beside his Mentor as they strolled from the room, he glanced up. "So which one are you?"

Three years later...

Chapter Nine

The delivery girl slicked on some lip gloss, then flipped up the visor. She clambered down, slid open the side door of the van, located the correct bags of Chinese take-out, and hurried up the walkway. *I hope that cute guy from last time answers the door,* she thought. Her heart fluttered when Griffin appeared, holding the screen ajar with one foot.

"Hey. How ya' doing?" He nodded as he took the bags and placed them inside the door on the bench. "How much is it?"

"Twenty-six, eighty-two," she said with a bright smile, tossing her hair over one shoulder.

"Okay. Here you go." He handed her the money. "Thanks. You're supposed to keep the change." Starting to close the screen, he stopped when she nonchalantly blocked it with her elbow.

"So ... um ... where do you go to school? Centennial?" she asked, anxious to keep the conversation going.

"No, I'm home-schooled." Griffin leaned against the doorframe, his hands shoved into his pockets. "A sophomore." He smiled down at her, his brown eyes crinkling at the corners. "What about you?"

Her stomach tingled. "I'm going to be a junior this year. So does your mom teach you or what?"

"Nah, my dad does."

"I do what, Fin?" asked Basil as he stepped out of his study and joined them in the entryway.

"Teach me at home," said Griffin over his shoulder.

"Oh. That." He smiled to himself and began rummaging through the bags.

"And what does your father do?" *Man, even the dad's good-looking,* she thought.

"He's an angel. So am I." Griffin grinned. "Cool, huh?"

"Wh ...what?"

"We're a type of angel. My dad and I." He straightened and flapped his arms up and down to illustrate his point.

Dropping a spring roll back into the sack, Basil reached over and pinned Griffin's hands to his side, yanking him away from the door. "What the bloody he ... heck are you doing?" he said under his breath. Smiling, he continued loudly, "my apologies. It's only a silly family gag, miss. Please ignore him." Basil elbowed Griffin further down the hall, trying to ignore his snickering. "Well, we'd best let you get back to work. Thank you." He nodded good-bye and shut the door on the bewildered girl. Gathering up the bags in one hand, he turned with a scowl.

"Hey, it's just a joke." Still laughing, Griffin flapped his arms a few more times as he lead the way to the kitchen, the salty sweet aroma of chow mein wafting around them.

"Wave them again, and I'm duct-taping them together."

"Bring it on!" He grinned up at his Mentor, dodging a cuff to his head.

Basil dumped the bags on the kitchen table. "Griffin, I'm serious! I want you to stop this nonsense before someone takes you literally."

"Oh, come on, Basil! Do you really think people are going to believe that angels exist? And that they live in middle-class neighborhoods and order Chinese take-out?"

"Griffin!"

"All right. All right." He pasted an expression of mock seriousness on his face. "I understand, Basil. And I'm sorry, Basil. And I won't do it again, Basil," he chanted as he unpacked the food.

"Cheeky brat."

Basil's Journal: Monday, August 15th

I'll be relieved when he outgrows this 'we're angels' routine. Until then, I'm stocking up on duct tape.

Griffin's Journal: Monday, August 15th

I am so ordering Chinese again this week. That girl's cute!

Basil always freaks about my angel jokes. Like humans would ever believe me. Anyway, the only ones that should be offended are the Winged Wonders.

Griffin's Journal: Tuesday, August 16th

Crap. Should have been more careful about that Winged Wonders comment. Got chewed out this morning from Basil for saying it at breakfast. I was just kidding around, but Basil's old-fashioned. Respect toward celestial angels is a big deal in our home.

Which I don't get. I mean, I don't see *them* around helping us out!

As reward for my cheek (that's what Basil calls it; I call it a consequence for being a smartmouth), I have to clean up the backyard. Which takes forever because we have so much training gear scattered all over it. Not to mention that mud puddle that we made our first month together.

Weird. Feels like I've lived two different lives: My years (more like my captivity) with Nicopolis and the last three years with Basil. Or maybe it's two different Griffins. Once in a while, I re-read my earlier journal entries (yes, Basil, I'm glad you made me write those) and realize how messed up I was.

Wonder if I still am?

I dream about him sometimes. The psycho. Of course, I wouldn't call it a dream. More like a nightmare. Which it was.

ၓ

"I'll start a fire break," said Griffin, stumbling a step from the force of their landing. Smoke from the grassland fire swirled around them, dimming the afternoon sun as the wind pushed the blaze toward the city's outlying neighborhood.

Basil scanned the surrounding backyards. "I don't believe anyone can see us in this smoke. And be careful. Grass fires are tricky. With these high winds, you can lose control before you know it."

Griffin rolled his eyes. "Basil, I know what I'm doing. It's like our fourth one this summer. You don't have to lecture me about safety all the time." He started to leave when Basil grabbed his arm and yanked him up short.

"I don't care if it's our bloody fortieth one," he growled. "All it takes is one careless move and you could be seriously injured. Or worse. So indulge me." He gave Griffin a shake. "You may be an Earth and Fire, but that does not make you totally impervious."

Griffin began to argue, and then closed his mouth at Basil's expression. "Okay, okay. I'll be careful. Can I go now?"

"Go."

Without another word, Griffin spun around and raced off, picking up speed as he ran across the field bordering the subdivision. As he neared the uneven line of flames, Fire erupted from his left hand. Without breaking stride, he veered and sprinted parallel to the inferno. His Fire streamed down his fingers, trailing behind him as he laid a blazing line through clumps of grass and brush.

"Ow!" he yelped, hopping on one foot. "Stupid cactus." He coughed as he bent over and yanked a spine out of his ankle. Giving his hand a shake, he started off again, gasping for breath as he struggled up the slope, his arm beginning to cramp from the Element. He stopped by a dirt road. That should be enough, he thought, then a grin spread across his sooty face as he looked back.

Basil appeared through the smoke, following Griffin's path. Marching across the field as Water poured from his fingertips, he hosed down the fire break, creating a barrier of muddy ground and soggy grasses. "Well done, Tiro," he called over the wind. He smiled as he walked up, wiping his hand dry on his jeans. "That should slow it down."

"Thanks," panted Griffin, clasping his hands on the top of his head. Taking a deep breath, he coughed again. "It's hard holding my Fire while—" He froze and stared down the road. "Oh, crap!"

Basil whirled around. "By the Light!"

Fire trucks roared toward them, already only a few yards away, their sirens inaudible over the wind and fire. As Basil and Griffin watched, the trucks skidded to a halt, the sand billowing up in a cloud and blinding them.

At that moment, Griffin lost sight of everything, except the distant glow of the firestorm. He heard Basil shouting and felt his Mentor tug at his elbow, then nothing. Squinting through the haze, he hesitated. He gasped when a gloved hand grabbed him.

"Oh, no, you don't," said an angry voice, the helmet casting a shadow on the firefighter's face. "Over to the truck. Now!" The man squeezed Griffin's arm in a tight vise and hauled him around to the back of the vehicle. He shoved him down on the back step. "Sit there and don't even twitch!"

"Sir, I was just trying to—" began Griffin.

"I'd shut up if I were you," said the man. He glanced over his shoulder as the other fighters crowded around, snatching their tools out of the truck. "Did you call the police?" he asked one of them.

"Already on their way. Look, we're going out there. You got him?"

"Yeah, I got him." The fireman took a step back as the others hurried toward the inferno. He glared down at Griffin. "I should be out there, too. Helping my buddies. Instead, I have to baby-sit you until the cops get here."

"But I didn't do anything!"

The fireman snorted. "Sure you did. You managed to burn almost four acres of state parkland, you endangered an entire subdivision, and you forced two teams into a hazardous situation."

Licking his lips, Griffin grimaced at the taste of salt from sweat and ash. I don't believe it, he thought. They think *I* started the fire! He slumped back against the truck and pushed his hair off his forehead, leaving a black streak across his brow like war paint. I gotta get out of here. If I could just get a running start, maybe I could take off without him seeing me. And where's Basil? I can't believe he just left me! He peeked out of the corner of his eye as the fireman stepped around the truck, craning his neck as he watched his team. For a moment, the air darkened as another cloud of smoke billowed overhead.

Griffin jumped to his feet and bolted; he stumbled once, almost going down, but caught himself and surged forward. He ran, his legs pumping, the man right on his heels and shouting at him. Just as the firefighter's fingers ghosted down the back of his tee shirt, Griffin launched himself into the air.

And vanished.

The firefighter careened to a halt. He spun on his heels, his head swiveling around as he checked every direction. "What the ...?" he murmured to himself.

ഌശ

Griffin crashed to the ground in his backyard, falling on his hands and knees. With a groan, he collapsed and rolled over, fighting for air. Finally catching his breath, he wiped the sweat out of his eyes and turned his head at the sound of the screen creaking open.

"Why, there you are," said Basil, sauntering past with a glass of iced tea in one hand, his hair spiky from a recent shower. "I was wondering what was keeping you." He took a sip and headed to the bench, sitting down with a contented sigh.

"They thought I had started the fire," wheezed Griffin. He coughed again and sat up, glaring at Basil. "I almost got arrested!"

"But you didn't."

"Basil!"

The Mentor hid his smile at Griffin's exasperation. "Fin, you need to learn ways and means of getting out of situations like that, so I thought this might be a good practice for you. How to hide your true identity while on missions."

Griffin started to argue, than gave up. "Yeah, you're probably right." He snorted. "You know, life would be a lot easier if we could just ... you know ... be ourselves," he said, struggling to his feet and joining his Mentor on the bench.

Basil handed the rest of the cold drink to Griffin. "Lad, that's true for the whole world."

Basil's Journal: Friday, August 19th

Fin's been going through another growth spurt. (I should have known by the amount of food he's been consuming.) For the record, he is now 5 feet 11 inches and roughly 160 lbs. He was quite tickled with that news, until I *punished* him (his words) by dragging him to the shop for new clothes. Supposedly, I am the cruelest Mentor in the world.

I would rather deal with a twenty-car pileup. On the Interstate. During a blizzard. With food poisoning, even, rather than take a fifteen-year-old Tiro shopping. He whined the entire time and refused to purchase anything but jeans and tee shirts. Jeans, I might add, that hang halfway off his bum. He's going to look quite ridiculous during a rescue when his pants fall down.

Griffin's Journal: Monday, August 22nd

I saw a couple moving in across the street. I couldn't tell if they had any kids or not. They seemed pretty excited. I heard them talking about older neighborhoods and bungalow houses and being only a few blocks from the College of Colorado. Basil said we'd stop by in a few days and introduce ourselves

Told me he's bringing duct tape, too. He thinks he's so funny.

Katie's Journal: Tuesday, August 23rd

I've decided to start a new journal since I'm starting a new life. Just like pioneers when they moved out West. I miss my friends and Grandma, but Iowa was boring. Colorado's awesome and I can tell that I'm going to like High Springs. It's got a cool downtown and, best of all, mountains! Can't wait to try some of the trails out. Dad and I are going running later. We better go slow at first, or I'll hack up a lung. Still getting used to the altitude!

My high school is just four blocks south. And Dad's campus is just three blocks west. He and I might walk part of the way together once in a while.

Hope I make some friends. Never been the new girl before.

I miss Bear. A lot!

I better go help Mom unpack the kitchen or we'll be ordering Chinese again.

Chapter Ten

Basil's Journal: Friday, August 26th

WE MET OUR NEW NEIGHBORS TODAY: Lewis and Helen Heflin. Their daughter, Katie, is about Griffin's age. Lewis is a new professor at the College. Comparative Religions and World Cultures. They were relieved to have found a home in this neighborhood as the school term begins shortly for both father and daughter.

Griffin was disturbingly well-behaved. Quiet. Polite.

I don't think it was my duct tape threat.

Griffin's Journal: Friday, August 26th

I just met this girl. The one whose family moved in across the street. Her name's Katie Heflin and she's about my age. She's a sophomore at the high school downtown. She was kind of quiet, but really nice. We only talked for a few minutes, standing on her porch. Basil didn't want to bother them since they're still unpacking. We took them some scones. (Scones, Basil? Are you kidding?) Anyway, Katie's really cute. I think her eyes were blue. No, green. Bluish-green. Really blond hair—almost looks white. Straight, but not long. Just to her shoulders. She's shorter than me.

Katie's Journal: Saturday, August 27th

Perfect! Just what I need! There's a dweeb across the street. He and his dad came by yesterday. I think the dad is Griffin and the son is Basil. Or is it the other way around? Anyway, their last name is Raine. The dad was nice, but the son kept staring at me. He didn't seem able to make normal conversation.

Probably because he's home-schooled.

Mom thought Mr. Raine was handsome and we both liked his English accent. Dad kept teasing her—said Mom liked him because he was tall and had hair. Dad always makes jokes about his bald head.

I'm glad Griffin (or is it Basil?) isn't going to my school. I can just see him following me around and being annoying.

He is cute, though.

ꝏ

"Keep going!" shouted the workman over the growl of the truck's engine as he stood behind the bumper, waving at his partner high in the driver's seat.

Nodding, the driver tapped the pedal, inching the massive vehicle backwards toward the loading dock. As he wrestled with the steering wheel, he felt a searing pain shoot across his chest and down his arm; his knee jerked spasmodically, slamming his foot down on the gas and sending the truck roaring backwards toward the workman.

A shadow flitted across the asphalt.

Arriving like a miniature tornado, Griffin launched himself at the man, shoving him out of harm's way. They tumbled to the ground in a heap as the huge tires rolled past, just missing them. The truck smashed into the platform with a metallic crunch, the engine screaming in protest before dying

They looked at each other, and then Griffin scrambled to his feet, wincing at his scraped elbow. He checked the wound, then blotted it on his tee shirt as he hunted for Basil.

"Hey, kid! You okay?" asked the man as he clambered up, gripping the lip of the loading dock for balance, his face colorless. "Holy cow, you saved my life!"

"Yeah. Well. It's what I do," said Griffin absently. "You didn't see another guy around, did you? Tall? White hair?"

"Didn't see anything except the ass end of that truck!" The workman grimaced and gripped his stomach, a greenish cast around his mouth. "Oh, man, I think I'm going to hurl!" Slapping his hand across his mouth, he raced inside the building, the restroom door slamming shut behind him.

I don't blame the guy, thought Griffin as he watched him sprint away, then swiveled his head at Basil's sharp whistle. He hurried around to the front of the truck and found his Mentor balanced on the cab's step, leaning in the open window, one hand splayed on the motionless driver's chest.

"What's going on?"

Snapping his cell phone shut, Basil shoved it in his pocket. "Heart attack," he said without turning his head. "I think I can keep it pumping until the paramedics get here. Is the other one safe?"

"Yeah, the guy's fine, except for the vomiting thing. But I tore my elbow up again."

Frowning, Basil glanced down. "That's because you tend to roll to the right when you take a fall. We'll drill this afternoon on that maneuver." He shifted his hand, using pulses of Might to stimulate the driver's heart.

Griffin rolled his eyes. No, he thought, *I'll* drill this afternoon on that maneuver. *You'll* sit on the patio with a cold drink while I throw myself around the backyard like an idiot. He brightened at the first scream of the ambulance.

"Go flag them down, Tiro."

Jogging around the truck, Griffin headed toward the chain link fence, waving the rescue vehicle through the gate. As it approached, he peered through the windshield, then whirled around and sprinted back to Basil.

"Hey, we got a problem!"

"We *have* a problem."

"No kidding. Those are the same emergency responders from our last two missions. They're sure to recognize us, especially you. Not a lot of tall, white-haired Brits around."

"By the Light!" swore Basil, craning his neck for a better view. "Right. We'll take off just as soon as they come around the front end. This gent's stable enough. Get ready." He hung on to the open window frame with one hand, keeping the other in place until the last moment. Griffin clambered up beside him, balancing on one foot as he clasped the side mirror. As the paramedics' voices grew louder, Basil nodded to him. *Three, two, one,* he mouthed. Side by side, they leaped up into the air, flipping backwards off the step, and then vanished in a blast of hot wind.

Katie's Journal: Monday, August 29th

Now that was weird.

Dad and I were finishing a run today when we came around the corner of our street. Couldn't see very well because of a parked car, but I thought I saw the Raines going up their steps. Like they had just come home.

It looked like the son was hurt or something. He was holding a handkerchief or something against his arm.

By the time we got where I could see better, they had gone inside. I asked Dad if he had seen them, but he hadn't.

Chapter Eleven

Katie's Journal: Wednesday, August 31st

I FEEL LIKE I'VE DONE NOTHING for the last two days except unpack boxes! Mom and I finally got a chance to go shopping for school clothes this morning, however. Got a great denim jacket!

I talked to that guy that lives across the street. He's not such a dweeb after all. Griffin (Basil's the dad—I figured it out while we were talking) came over this afternoon when I was getting our mail. Actually, he was checking his mailbox at the same time. We started talking about school, parents, regular stuff. Trying to have a polite conversation while practically yelling across the street. We both stopped and laughed at the same time, and then he just walked on over.

Funny. He doesn't walk in that floppy way that a lot of boys do. Like they don't have complete control over their arms and legs. He walks like he's ... older. Must be in sports; looks pretty athletic. Hard to tell with jeans and a tee shirt, but he has some muscle on his arms and chest. But not the kind jocks have. The kind farmers back in Iowa had.

I was going to ask him if he liked being home-schooled, but he suddenly jerked his head around like he heard something and said Ihavetogoanditwasnicetalkingwithyou all in one breath, and tore across the street, taking the steps two at a time. I saw his dad standing there, holding the screen open for him.

Was it something I said?

Basil's Journal: Wednesday, August 31st

We received an unexpected rescue call this afternoon. It would have been bloody helpful to know we were on rotation, thank you very much! Luckily, Griffin was just across the street and caught my whistle. I don't think the girl heard it. I have to hand it to the lad—he came a-running.

Unfortunately, as soon as he arrived, Command canceled the call.

Naturally, he was a royal pain about his flirtation with Miss Heflin being interrupted.

ꕥ

Basil turned off the grinder and busied himself scooping the grounds into the coffee machine. He watched out of the corner of his eye as Griffin marched into the kitchen, jerked open the refrigerator door, yanked out the pie, carried it to the table, snatched a fork out of the drawer and plopped down.

The Menor silently counted to ten. "You may leave this kitchen until you can return with a more civil manner," he said over his shoulder, rinsing the grinder out in the sink. When he didn't hear any movement, he looked over. Griffin sat glaring at him, his arms folded across his chest.

"Now, Tiro!"

Shoving his chair back, its wooden feet screeching against the floor, Griffin stomped out. Silence filled the adjoining room for a minute, then he returned, taking his seat with exaggerated care, a scowl still on his face. Basil flipped on the coffee maker and leaned against the counter as he finished drying his hands, his eyes unyielding as he stared at Griffin.

Griffin fidgeted under the scrutiny. He shifted sideways in his chair, picking at a nail for a few minutes before surrendering. "Sorry," he mumbled.

Basil nodded once, accepting the apology. "Command just informed me that we're now on call the entire night," he said as he fetched a fork and sat down. Sliding the pie plate to the center of the table, he dug in, inviting Griffin to join him. He took a bite, then made a face. "Hmmm... this would taste better warm."

"Lemme get it," Griffin said, holding both hands out flat. Basil lifted the pie plate and set it on his palms. They watched for a few moments until the fruit juices began bubbling, wisps of steam rising up.

"That should be enough. Thanks, Fin." Griffin laid the warm pan on the towel Basil had hastily snatched from the counter.

"The other Mentors and their Tiros were needed in Denver tonight," Basil told him. "Therefore, against my better judgment, I'm allowing you one cup of coffee with your pie."

"Two cups."

"Two, with lots of milk."

"One and a half. No milk."

"How about none?" offered Basil.

"You know, one cup is good." Griffin hopped up to fetch their mugs.

Basil sighed. "I'm so going to regret this."

Basil's Journal: Wednesday, August 31st (cont.)

When will I learn? One cup sends Griffin ricocheting off the walls for hours. Babbling nonstop. Then he started asking questions—the ones that are almost impossible to answer.

He wanted to know what would happen if more people knew about the Kellsfarne manuscript. I explained to him that knowledge of the manuscript's content is not perilous in itself. It's the belief in the legend that makes life complicated for Terrae Angeli. Especially if people start looking for signs. Because mortals truly want to believe in angelic beings.

Until one shows up.

Then he wanted to know why humans and Terrae Angeli were given free will and not the celestials? I reminded him that free will, the ability to choose for oneself, can be a burden as well as a gift.

Because some choices will break your heart.

ꕥ

The desk chair squealed as Griffin rocked back and forth. He sighed, and then leaned over and snatched a scrap of paper out of the trashcan. Folding it into a compact triangle, he balanced it on one corner and aimed, punting it with a flick of his fingers. It sailed across the room, straight toward the fireplace, bursting into flames before landing on the logs.

"No Elements in the house," murmured Basil, engrossed in his book. He turned another page and settled more comfortably on the sofa. After a while, registering the silence, he looked up and studied Griffin's face. What is he fretting about now? he thought. I swear, the lad's going to be the first Terrae Angelus in existence with an ulcer.

"Basil?"

"Fin."

"What happens? When an angel becomes mortal? I mean, does it ... hurt?"

The Mentor's heart twisted. "Yes. Yes, it's quite painful," he said reluctantly.

"Where would I go? To live?" Griffin toyed with a glass paperweight, spinning it around on the worn surface. "I guess I'd have to get a job. Or go to school or something."

Basil put down his book. "Thinking about the Proelium?"

Griffin shrugged. "Sixteen in two months, you know."

"First of all, you're acting as if you've failed already," he said, "which isn't going to happen. Second, you don't complete the Proelium the *instant* you turn sixteen. Yours will most likely be on or around the winter solstice. When one of the Senior Mentors is able to administer it. Third, no matter what happens, this is your home. For as long as you wish."

Griffin kept his eyes on the paperweight. "Promise?"

"I promise."

Chapter Twelve

Katie's Journal: Friday, September 6th

FIRST WEEK OF SCHOOL WASN'T TOO BAD. Centennial High is bigger than my old school, so lots of other new students. I met a really cute guy, a junior named Nash Baylor in AP math. He talked with me a few minutes at the end of the class. I have two classes and lunch with another new girl, Carlee Webb, so we hooked up. Don't have a lot in common, except our newbie status. She's really nice and funny, but talks a lot. Carlee kept pointing out all the good-looking guys. Every single one.

She offered to help me with history after I told her it was my worst subject. We might get together this weekend.

Mom wants me to go move the sprinkler. Why she's watering the lawn when summer's practically over is beyond me. This is Colorado. Shouldn't we be getting snow soon?

ฺ໓ଓ

Catching the screen door with her heel before it slammed behind her, Katie glanced idly across the street, then trotted down the steps and around to the spigot. She turned off the water, and then pulled the hose over to the final section of dry lawn, squishing back through the wet turf to the faucet. "Break down and get a sprinkler system, guys," she muttered to herself. As she edged around the tall shrub next to the house, she looked over and spotted Griffin striding down the street, a book bag slung across his chest.

Katie froze, and then eased back and scrunched down. Hidden behind the bush, she craned her neck, peeking through the branches as she studied Griffin—the way he moved, the fit of his dark tee shirt across his shoulders, his boyish features that would be called handsome in another year or two. Hmmm. Maybe I should say hi, she thought to herself. She took a deep breath and tucked her hair behind one ear. "Here goes nothing," she murmured and stepped around the shrubbery.

Directly into the path of the oscillating sprinkler.

"Holy crap," she squealed as the cold water doused her. Holding her arms over her head, she darted away, the spray chasing her as she scrambled to the other side of the lawn. Halfway across, she skidded on the wet grass and landed on her bottom.

Before she could move, a shadow fell across her.

"Are you okay?" asked Griffin as he reached down and clasped her arm.

Katie stared at his tanned hand against her pale skin for a moment, and then blinked as he lifted her to her feet. "Yeah. Just embarrassed." She swiped at her soaked jeans. "Stupid sprinkler." Her eyes widened in confusion as he tightened his grip and took a step back, pulling her with him.

Griffin pointed over her shoulder with his chin. "Incoming," he explained as another spray of water curled past them.

Katie laughed, shaking her head. Griffin grinned back, his smile as warm as the afternoon sun. Pushing his hair off his forehead, he let go and gestured toward the hose.

"Is that where you want it or can I move it for you? I don't mind a little water." His eyes twinkled.

"Nah, it's fine. Just needed to finish that last section." I feel like an idiot, she grumbled to herself. She scrubbed her hands on her pants, then nodded toward his book bag. "I thought you were home-schooled?"

"I am. But I had to do some work in the downtown library. Bas... I mean, Dad assigned me a research paper that takes more than the Internet can handle." Griffin stopped and made a face. "Makes me sound like a total geek," he said, a faint blush spreading across his face. Before Katie could answer, the front screen slapped open.

Helen Heflin trudged down the steps and along the walk, an overflowing recycle bin in her hands. "Hello, Griffin. How are you?" She smiled as she hoisted the crate more securely.

"Hi, Mrs. Heflin. Can I help?" he asked, elbowing his book bag to one side as he took the heavy container from her.

"Why, thank you, kind sir. Just put it on the curb at the end of the driveway, please." As he hauled it away, Helen cocked her head at her daughter. *Nice manners,* she mouthed. Katie rolled her eyes. When Griffin returned, she said, "I see Katie lost a battle with the sprinkler."

"It wasn't her fault. The sprinkler had it in for her—I could tell." As Helen laughed, Griffin noticed the close resemblance between mother and daughter, right down to the same pale hair and blue-green eyes.

They all turned and watched as a dusty SUV honked once, then pulled into the gravel driveway. Lewis Heflin clambered out and dragged a bulging briefcase from the back seat. Noticing the threesome in the yard, he loosened his tie and sauntered over. "Why, hello there, Gregory," he said.

"It's *Griffin,*" said Helen out of the side of her mouth.

"Oh, sorry. I meant Griffin."

"Sir." Griffin nodded once and held out his hand.

Lewis raised his eyebrows in surprise. "*Sir,* huh? Now that's refreshing to hear."

"Would you like to stay for dinner?" asked Helen. "We usually order pizza on Fridays as soon as Lewis gets home. And we always have too many leftovers."

Griffin's heart skipped a beat. Before answering, he glanced at Katie. At her slight nod and smile, he brightened. "Yes, please! I just need to check in with my dad and drop off my bag. Be right back."

While her parents debated pizza toppings, Katie waited as Griffin hurried across the lawn, a smile on her lips. It faded as she watched him head into the path of the sprinkler. As she opened her mouth to shout a warning, he marched through the spray, breaking into a jog crossing the street.

He became bone dry after four strides.

Griffin's Journal: Friday, September 6th

I screwed up. Big time.

Basil wouldn't let me have dinner with Katie and her parents. He made me go over and tell them that we already had plans. They were nice about it and said maybe next week. I wasn't sure if Katie was relieved or not. I think she was. Can't tell if she likes me or was just being polite.

Anyway, Basil wanted to talk with me when I got back about why I couldn't go. He said something about us being on standby. But I was pissed at him so I ignored him and ran upstairs. I heard him yelling at me to come back, but I just slammed my door.

It's been really quiet downstairs.
Scary quiet.

ꕥ

Basil gripped the newel post; his lips moved silently as he counted to one hundred, then hollered. "Griffin! Downstairs! Now!" At the sound of thumping feet, he stalked through the archway into the living room and waited, his hands on his hips.

Griffin appeared in the doorway. "Um ... you wanted me?" he began, and then snapped his mouth shut when Basil spun around.

"There's a fine line between expressing your frustration over a situation and downright disrespect. A line you just crossed, Tiro," said Basil, his blue eyes stormy. "Don't you *ever* act that way again!"

Griffin swallowed as he shifted from foot to foot. "Okay." He glanced away, chewing on the inside of his mouth, his heart starting to pound.

"And look at me when I'm speaking to you." Griffin jerked his head up, his eyes front and center. "Now, if you've a question about an order, then ask me. And until I'm through explaining, you will stand there and listen. You can go sulk when I'm finished. Do you understand me?"

"Yes, sir," Griffin whispered, trying to control his breathing. Okay. Don't freak out. It's just Basil. All he does is yell. He yells and then it's over with.

"Good. Because I will not tolerate that kind of behavior from any Tiro of mine." Basil took a calming breath and exhaled. "Now, if you'll excuse me," he said after a moment and marched toward the door, heading for his study. "I need to finish a report."

Griffin squeezed to one side of the archway, his eyes fixed on the floor. "Sorry I was rude," he mumbled as his Mentor brushed past.

A wry smile on his face, Basil stopped and turned around. "Apology accepted. And Griffin? I'm not angry at *you.* I'm angry at your behavior. Do you understand the difference?"

"Yes, sir."

"Right." Basil disappeared into his study, closing the door behind him. Slumping against the wall, Griffin sighed and scrubbed at his face, then lowered his trembling hands, staring at them. Fire, I hate it when he chews me out, he thought. I know he's not going to do anything. So why do I always think he might? Like one day I'll make him so pissed that he'll just lose it? And haul off and hit me. He jumped when Basil opened the door.

"Fin!" he called out, then looked up in surprise. "Oh, there you are." He frowned. "Why are you still standing there, lad?"

Griffin shrugged, unable to look Basil in the eye.

"Having a bit of a meltdown, eh?" said the Mentor with a trace of a wink. "Well, be sure to clean it up afterwards. And then start dinner, would you?"

Griffin chuckled weakly, grateful for the jesting, the strain easing between them. "Whadda you want?" he asked, pushing away from the wall and heading toward the kitchen.

"I'm not sure," Basil called after him. "Oh, and I just received word we're no longer on standby. Since we have a free evening, we could... order pizza."

Griffin's groan of frustration echoed down the hall.

Chapter Thirteen

Katie's Journal: Saturday, September 7th

MOM TOTALLY EMBARRASSED ME YESTERDAY!!!

We have this agreement that she won't do things like that! I don't like her inviting other kids to come over for dinner or whatever. Like I need her help making friends? I felt like a three-year-old. With my mom setting up a play date with the other babies.

Griffin couldn't make it. Said his dad had already made plans. He seemed bummed about it, but was trying to be polite. Thanked my mom and everything for inviting him. Told me he would see me around.

Basil's Journal: Saturday, September 7th

A fifteen-year-old Tiro.

A pretty girl across the street.

Oy vey.

Katie's Journal: Monday, September 9th

What a great way to start the week! Uncle Gordon's coming from Iowa to Denver with a load, so he's going to bring Bear with him! I hated leaving him with Grandma until we got settled, but Dad said it's easier to get all moved in without a dog underfoot. I think Bear would have been fine, but whatever.

Can't wait for Thursday!!!

Griffin's Journal: Wednesday, September 11th

I got to go on some solo missions this week! Totally by myself. I got to take the call from Command and everything.

Of course, they were barely missions. More like people just needed a helping hand. Still, Basil said it was good practice for me—assessing a situation and how to solve it. Figuring out how to use my abilities without looking like I'm using my abilities.

He really liked the way I solved the second mission. The guy must have been so excited to bring his new baby home that he locked the keys in the car. I walked by and asked if they needed any help. When he pointed out his problem, I reached over and pretended to jiggle the handle at the same time I used just enough Might to pop the lock. My Might use still sucks, but it worked this time! Then I told him that it was unlocked on my side and opened the door.

As he was tucking the baby into the child seat, I heard his wife tell him not to worry so much. That she heard somewhere every baby has a guardian angel.

Nice job keeping quiet about us, Thomas Aquinas.

Katie's Journal: Thursday, September 12th

Carlee just left. She helped me study for our big history test Monday. Carlee's a nut! It's kind of fun to have a friend who's so different. She's always saying the goofiest things and is totally boy crazy. I think a couple of guys in class like her. She teased me about Nash Baylor. She said that she heard that he thinks I'm cute and really smart. I have to admit: I liked hearing that since he's one of the coolest guys in school. And he's a junior and I'm just a sophomore!

Dad's going to get Bear after supper. Since he can't bring his rig into our neighborhood, Uncle Gordon's going to meet Dad at a truck stop along the highway. I wanted to go, but the SUV's still in the shop, so he's taking Mom's Bug. There's no way an Irish wolfhound and I would both fit.

He's not called Bear for nothing!

I'm going to go wait on the porch.

Basil's Journal: Thursday, September 12th

You cannot write this stuff—it's just Real Life.

As we were unloading the Saab this evening from yet another grocery store trip, Lewis Heflin pulled into his driveway in a very tiny car with a very large dog. Opening the passenger door, Katie flung her arms around what was obviously a beloved family member. It was a warm and tender scene.

Then the dog sensed Griffin and me. And as I once explained to Griffin, no creature in this world loves Terrae Angeli more than dogs. Except babies.

All I can say is that Bear, despite his size, can really move. As he charged across the street toward us, with all three Heflins in pursuit, I did the only thing a Mentor could do.

I placed my Tiro between the dog and myself, ordered him to hold his position, and beat a hasty retreat. Out of the corner of my eye, I saw Griffin go sailing.

By the time the Heflins caught up, and I made a reluctant reappearance, Bear was sprawled on Griffin, licking his hair with delight. All we could see of him were his feet.

It's a good thing he knows how to take a fall.

Griffin's Journal: Thursday, September 12th

Just discovered that dog slobber makes a powerful hair gel. You can get all sorts of crazy styles. If you can stand the smell. Took a while to shampoo it out.

I felt bad for Katie. She was so embarrassed. It wasn't a big thing. Basil and I deal with that insane behavior from dogs all the time.

Wonder how dogs sense us. Do we smell different from humans? Sound different?

I'll stop by Saturday and see how her dog is doing. Joke about cushioning Bear's landing.

I think we're on call tonight. Hope it's not something boring.

ജ്ഞ

"Hey, I know who you two are!" said a creaky voice. They whirled around as the man tottered down the poorly lit sidewalk toward them, wispy hair sticking out from beneath his knitted cap.

"I thought you had escorted him back inside his apartment," Basil muttered.

Before Griffin could answer, the old man arrived. "You're them. I knew it! When you came outta nowhere to help me." He cackled with glee.

Griffin glanced up at his Mentor and shrugged. Basil opened his mouth to protest, but the man continued.

"Yessiree. You're those guardian angel guys. The ones on motorcycles, right? Well, maybe not motorcycles. A club or something. Patrolling the streets at night. With leather jackets, I think. And those flat hats like the Frenchies wear." He flashed a toothless grin and pushed his thick glasses higher on his nose. Leaning closer, he peered at Griffin, his smile dimming. "'Course, this one seems a bit young for it, don't you think, mister?"

"It's most likely you have us confused with—" Basil began, then stopped when Griffin grabbed his arm, and began steering him away.

"Why, yes, sir!" Griffin said. "That's *exactly* who we are. The guardian angel guys." He shushed Basil, who started to protest, and kept edging away. "Glad to have helped, but we need to move along. No. No thanks are necessary. Go back inside, stay safe, and no more late-night trips to the dumpster."

As the old man shuffled back to the entrance of his building, a sudden breeze snatched the cap off his head and swept it a few feet away. As he bent to retrieve it, he thought he heard the sound of boyish laughter on the wind and a stern voice scolding.

Katie's Journal: Saturday, September 14th

Sometimes something bad turns into something good. Like Thursday, when Bear plowed into Griffin. We must have looked like the biggest bunch of dorks in the world. But he just laughed, even with Bear's slobber all over his hair.

He did a really nice thing after we got Bear off—he knelt down and gave my dog a hug. After that, Bear calmed right down and sat. Usually, he's bouncing all around (he's only two years old—still a puppy), but he was really a good boy after that. Well, after he attacked our neighbors.

Mr. Raine was nice about it, too. Although he looked silly when he ran inside. Maybe he's scared of dogs or something. Anyway, my parents are going to have them over for a barbeque lunch tomorrow after Mom gets back from church to apologize again.

So. How did the bad thing turn into a good thing? Well, Griffin came by this morning. He said he wanted to see if Bear was all right. When I answered the door, Bear started going berserk again. Then Griffin just laid his hand on my dog's head and said *be still.* And he was! Amazing!

So we sat on the porch with Bear and talked. About our favorite books. What countries we would like to visit. Our parents. The mountains. What it would be like to have brothers and sisters. If there's other creatures in the universe beside humans. Is there really a God? (He sure acted surprised when I told him I didn't think so.) Would it be more fun to be able to fly or be invisible? Why some parts of the world have so many problems. What we want to be when we're adults.

It was like we were friends.

Chapter Fourteen

Griffin's Journal: Saturday, September 14th

BASIL WILL KILL ME IF HE FINDS ME UP THIS LATE, but I can't sleep. I think Katie likes me. We talked a long time today about all sorts of things. She wonders about the same things I do.

Except our futures.

She thinks she might want to be an astronaut when she grows up, but she's not sure. It must be weird not knowing what you're going to be when you're older. Not knowing why you're here on Earth. I wonder if there's ever been a Terrae Angelus who wanted to be something else. And why would they?

I found out (by accident, no matter what Basil thinks!) that Katie's bedroom window is right across the street from mine. Both on the second floor. I was getting undressed for bed and happened to look out and saw her cranking her window closed. I just watched for a second.

Talk about bad timing on my part.

ꟸ

Griffin yawned as he nudged his door open with his toe and paused inside the dark bedroom, yanking his shirt over his head. Wadding it into a ball, he aimed and sent it arching toward the plastic basket under the window, then rolled his eyes at the near miss. Scratching under one arm, he walked around his bed and snatched the tee off the floor. As he straightened up, he glanced out. His eyes widened; the shirt dangled unforgotten from his fingers. Katie stood framed in her bedroom window, her slender form hidden in pajamas pants and a College of Colorado sweatshirt. He watched as she pushed up her sleeves and tugged on the old casement handle with both hands, attempting to crank it shut.

As Griffin remained hidden in the dark, the night breeze drifted through the half-opened window, stirring one of the drapes. The fabric brushed against his bare shoulder and chest. His lips parted as a tingle ran down his spine and into his legs.

"And just what are you doing?"

Griffin jumped with a gasp, and then whirled around. Basil stood silhouetted in the open doorway. Oh, please don't turn on the lights, he prayed silently. She might see them and think I was watching her. "Just getting ready for bed," he said aloud.

Basil's eyes narrowed at the half-truth in Griffin's voice. Ambling into the room, he glanced around, and then walked over. As he halted by the window, he looked out, started to speak, then peered more closely. His mouth tightened as he observed Katie win the battle with her window and lower her blinds, the lights in her room flicking off a few moments later.

"Were you watching her?" he asked over his shoulder.

"I was getting my shirt off the floor. To put it in the basket." Griffin held it up as evidence before dropping it in.

"That's not what I asked you." He turned and folded his arms across his chest. "Were you watching Katie?"

"Yeah," Griffin admitted. "Pretty creepy of me, huh?"

"Especially dressed like that," said Basil, raising an eyebrow. "Or undressed, I should say."

Griffin winced in embarrassment, then edged past and snagged another shirt out of his dresser. As he slipped it over his head, he mumbled, "I don't see what the big deal is. She wasn't ... you know ... in her underwear or anything."

"It was improper of you and you know it," said Basil as he reached over and clicked on the bedside lamp. Lowering the window, he tugged the drapes firmly together, then gestured for Griffin to take a seat on the bed.

"Fin, having human acquaintances can be risky. It's so easy to let slip what we are, especially to a friend. Most are not able to handle the idea that we exist. So be cautious. Because no matter how much we try to blend in, we can't. Not perfectly. Our way of life is just too ... singular. If you wish to be friends with Katie, that's fine, as long as you can balance it."

"I understand," said Griffin, picking at the stitching on his quilt. "It's just that Katie's ... well, she's really ... nice."

"Are you interested in her as more than just as a friend? Maybe in a romantic sense?" At Griffin's awkward nod, Basil stepped closer to the bed, towering over his Tiro.

"Physically and emotionally, we *are* more like humans than celestial angels. Except we are created, not birthed. So it would stand to reason that we would have the same wants and desires, the same joys and fears as humans. Except for one difference."

"What's that?"

"That we choose not to act on those emotions as a mortal would. Always remember, you are a Terrae Angelus. That's *Angelus*," he emphasized. "Therefore I expect you to be a gentleman and act properly. All the time. In all ways."

"All right, all right, I get the message."

"And Fin? The next time you so much as change your *socks*, I want those drapes drawn. Understand?"

Griffin blushed.

ഇഗ

"Katie, carry the potato salad out. Griffin, would you take the iced tea pitcher? Careful, it's full." Helen Heflin finished seasoning the hamburger patties, picked up the tray, and followed the teens through the back door and out to the Heflin's shady backyard.

"Mr. Raine," she called over to Basil as he stood in the far corner with Lewis, admiring the newly installed fountain. "I forgot to ask if you and Griffin eat meat. I have both here—veggie burger or ground beef?"

"I believe I'll try the beef, thank you, but Griffin won't eat meat. And please call me Basil." He hurried over to help with the platter, rolling up the sleeves of his shirt. Helen shooed him away.

"Go sit with Lewis. He doesn't get a lot of man talk in this house."

Lewis smiled as Basil joined him, both taking seats in lawn chairs under the shade of the enormous cottonwood tree. The professor smoothed his dark goatee, then clasped his hands behind his head and sighed contentedly. "I should be helping with lunch, but Helen's giving me the day off. Since the term's begun, I get a little more pampering." Lewis grinned at his wife and blew her a kiss.

Katie made a gagging sound as she walked over. "Okay. Gross," she said, serving her father iced tea.

"Actually, your mother and I don't even like each other. We just do things like that to drive you insane. Is it working yet?" asked Lewis straight-faced.

Basil laughed. Katie rolled her eyes and placed another iced tea on a nearby table and headed back to Griffin.

"Thank you, miss," Basil called after her, picking up the glass and swirling it around, clinking the ice against the sides. "Your daughter is charming, Lewis. My son is quite smitten." He chuckled. "He's a late bloomer when it comes to the young ladies. I'm afraid she may find him a bit awkward."

"Well, I have a feeling the attraction is mutual," said Lewis. "And this is new to Katie, too. Helen and I are old-fashioned parents." He paused and took a sip of his drink. "We haven't allowed her to date or have a boyfriend until this year. I think fifteen's soon enough." Lewis glanced over at the twosome teasing Bear with a slice of cheese. "They don't need to grow up too quickly," he added softly. Basil raised his glass in agreement.

"Say. Helen was curious about your first names. They're quite unusual in this day and age," said Lewis, changing the subject.

At that moment, Helen sat down on a nearby chair, blowing her blonde bangs out of her eyes. "Oh, good, I heard Lewis asking about your names. And don't tell me it has to do with the sixties." They laughed at her charming bluntness.

"No. Not at all," said Basil. "*Basil* is an old family name. And as I have roots in Wales as well as England, *Griffin* seemed appropriate."

"Is, or was, his mother British, too?" Helen asked.

"No, she was not," he replied, shifting in his chair. An uncomfortable silence followed.

"Mom, I think these are done," Katie called from the barbeque through a cloud of smoke. She poked at the burgers with a spatula, the juices dripping onto the hot grill with a sizzle.

"I'll get them, Helen. Everyone, go sit down," said Lewis. After a few minutes, he joined the rest of the party gathered at the table under the large umbrella. Bear watched forlornly from his dog bed on the corner of the patio.

As dishes were circulated around the group, Griffin paused, his fork hovering over the mound of patties. "Which ones are the veggie burgers, Mrs. Heflin?"

"The ones on the left side, dear. Are you a vegetarian?"

"No, just a weird allergy," he said, passing the tray to Katie. "I can't eat meat from any land animals. Seafood's okay."

She frowned. "I've never heard of that before."

Griffin shrugged. "What's even stranger is that Dad's the opposite. He can't eat anything from the ocean or even lakes or streams," he said, swallowing a bit of burger. "Hey, these aren't bad."

"So what happens if you eat meat? I mean land animals?" Katie asked.

"Have you ever eaten ice cream really fast and gotten a brain freeze?" asked Griffin. "It's like that, but even more painful. But it usually passes pretty fast." He grinned around another mouthful. "You should have seen my dad a few months ago when he accidentally got some of my tuna salad. I thought he was going to pass out in the restaurant. He bit his lip so hard it bled all over his shirt and the tablecloth. Even dripped on the floor."

"Thank you, *son*," said Basil dryly. "I'm sure the Heflins enjoyed hearing that tale whilst eating."

Griffin waved at him, safe on the opposite side of the table. "No problem, *Dad*."

"I'm allergic to housework myself," said Helen as she looked around the table. "So when everyone's finished, the adults will enjoy the rest of the afternoon out here while you two have kitchen duty." As Katie began to protest, Helen raised a hand. "No need to thank me," she said with a wicked smile.

ꙮ

"Wanna rinse or load?" asked Katie.

"I'll rinse. I'm not sure how you want them loaded."

As Griffin began scrubbing each dish, his head bowed over his task, Katie waited to one side. Trying not to be obvious, she studied him; noting the way his hair varied in shades from auburn to espresso; it curled slightly at the nape of his neck. Her eyes traveled down his face. I wonder how he got that, she thought, noticing an old scar near the edge of his lower lip. She blinked in confusion when Griffin turned and handed her the first plate.

After a few minutes of awkward silence and industrious labor, Katie tucked the final bowl inside the dishwasher and shut the door as

Griffin wiped the sink clean. Reaching for the towel at the same time, they froze, their hands outstretched, and looked at each other.

"Go ahead," they said simultaneously.

"No, that's all right." They spoke again in unison.

"You first," they said in chorus.

Laughing, Griffin picked up the towel and held it out to Katie. "Oh, no, *ladies* first."

She took it from him with a smirk. "I'm surprised you didn't offer to dry them for me."

"Do you want me to?" he asked, half-jokingly.

"Only if I can dry yours," Katie teased back.

They gazed at each other, and then Griffin stepped closer and plucked the towel out of her hand. Draping it over his open palms, he held it out and waited, his eyes still locked with hers while his heart began thumping against his ribs. As Katie laid her slender hands in his, he wrapped first one, then the other, bundling them in the terry cloth. Rubbing gently, Griffin concentrated as he heated the thick fabric between his palms. *Not too much Element or she'll notice. Just enough.* He started to speak when muffled voices announced the adults outside the back door.

Griffin swallowed and let go of Katie's hands, pulling the warmed towel free and tossing it on the counter. "I ... um ..." he began, than stopped.

"Yeah. Me, too. I mean ...," Katie faltered, tucking her hair nervously behind her ear.

They stood looking everywhere, but at each other.

Griffin's Journal: Sunday, September 15th

I really like Katie. I mean I really, really like her.

So what do I do next?

Katie's Journal: Sunday, September 15th

Do I like him *that* way? I think I do.

I never notice the shape of his mouth. Until today.

Chapter Fifteen

Basil's Journal: Sunday, September 15th

CONCERT AT ROCK GARDEN AMPHITHEATER. Late evening.

There were just too many of them. When the band invited people up on the stage, a riot broke out. We tried to rescue as many as we could from being injured. In the end, it was all I could do to rescue Griffin.

I was up on the edge of the stage, preventing people from being crushed, vaguely aware of Griffin a few yards away, clearing a path for the police through the audience. Individuals were being trampled underfoot.

I saw the mob suddenly surge forward, Griffin struggling to keep on his feet. He Might-blocked a few at first, but couldn't maintain his concentration. I lost him as he went down.

Leaping from the stage, I blasted a jet of air into the crowd. I was able to push the rioters back and away from the victims; many lay groaning on the floor.

I finally spotted Griffin struggling to his feet, shaking his head and blinking. He looked a bit battered and probably got his bell rung. Wiping his bloody nose on his shirttail, he gave me a thumbs-up and a nod, then turned to assist the nearest person.

Good lad.

Katie's Journal: Monday, September 16th

Carlee Webb is dead! She is such a flirt! This afternoon, we went to the coffee shop near school to celebrate making it through our history test. I'd never been before, but she went last week and said it was cool because a lot of college kids hung out there, too. It's called Oh-Be-Joyful. I think it's named after a mountain pass or something.

Anyway, we were sitting there, lucky to have a table because it was packed, having a mocha latte and talking. Well, Carlee was talking, I was nodding and listening.

Then it happened. Carlee stopped yakking and said a real hottie just walked in. Since my back was to the door, I assumed it was another college boy. But she said he looked our age and that she was going to go over to the counter where he was waiting for his order and say hi.

One thing I'll say about Carlee: she is fearless. Mom calls it something else, but Mom's behind the times.

Anyway, she squeezed past me and headed over. I was sitting there waiting when I heard Griffin! Laughing!

I looked around. Carlee was over there messing with my ... with my ...

My I-don't-know-yet.

Then Carlee said something and they both looked at me. He seemed happy to see me. They both came over and we sat and talked for a while.

It was so weird! Griffin and I couldn't talk about the stuff we liked because Carlee was there. I hadn't told Carlee about Griffin, just that he was a neighbor, so she felt free to flirt with him. Griffin kept looking more and more confused because my friend was coming on to him and I wasn't doing anything.

Finally, he had to leave. After he said good-bye, Carlee gushed on and on about him. She said that since I wasn't interested, she might go after him.

Like he's a trophy to win.

Griffin and I are just starting to like each other. Should I tell Carlee that I'm interested in him?

Oh, and by the way, I didn't like the way she kept touching his arm every time she said something to him!

Griffin's Journal: Monday, September 16th

So does she or doesn't she? I thought she did, but then this afternoon at Oh-Be-Joyful, she acted like she barely knew me. Like we had just met or something. Carlee's nice. She's cute and I like her red hair. Plus she's really funny.

But she isn't Katie.

Chapter Sixteen

Griffin's Journal: Wednesday, September 18th

I HAVEN'T SEEN KATIE SINCE MONDAY at the coffee shop. I think she's avoiding me. I just saw her leave with Bear to go for a walk—I know she takes him around the block to the empty field behind our house. It's a safe place to let him off the leash and run out some of his crazy energy.

I think our backyard needs cleaning.

ꕥ

"Bear," yelled Katie. "Bear, come here. Now!" Dust puffed up as the dog careened around her, a shaggy grey-brown tornado, first one direction, and then the other. As he wheeled and charged her, Katie yanked down the sleeves of her worn hoodie and steeled herself for the assault. She squealed as Bear almost barreled into her, then swerved aside at the last instant and raced past her, his high-pitched woof reflecting the puppy in him. He turned and skidded to a halt halfway across the field and bowed down with his rump in the air. *Come and play with me.*

"You're so silly! Come. Here." It's hard to make a dog obey when you're laughing, thought Katie. As Bear ignored her and trotted over to investigate an enticing bush, she spied Griffin moving about his backyard. Looks like he's doing some work or something. Do I say hi or what? Act like everything's okay?

"Why does everything have to be so ... complicated?" she said to herself. Unnoticed, Bear stood motionless, neck arched and eyes fixed intently on the shrub before him.

The rabbit bolted away, its white tail stark against its brown hindquarters and its back feet a blur. The wolfhound yelped with delight, his feet scrabbling for purchase on the dry ground before he settled into his stride. Desperate to fill his mouth with soft, warm bunny, Bear became deaf to every sound as both animals sprinted across the field toward the far street.

"Bear," Katie shrieked in horror. "Bear! No!" She sprinted a few feet, stumbled and almost went down. Catching herself, she ran, the leash flopping in her grip and the metal clip stinging her hand with every stride. Too far ahead of her, Bear galloped full out, intent on catching his prey, the rabbit speeding up, frantic to lengthen the distance between itself and the monster behind it. The line of traffic in the street ahead roared past, unaware of the two animals hurtling blindly toward them. Katie screamed soundlessly in her head when a car hit the rabbit first. "Oh, please," she moaned, tears blinding her as she ran. "Please stop him!"

Bear's front paws never made it past the curb.

Griffin tackled the dog around his neck and shoulders in mid-air, his momentum sending them both tumbling through the tall grass bordering the street. He slammed into the ground, grunting as Bear crashed down on top of him, trying to claw free. Each swipe of the dog's ragged nails dug into Griffin's chest and stomach, tearing through shirt and skin. Gritting his teeth, he slung a leg over the squirming dog. "Easy, boy—it's just me." As Bear calmed down, he eased his stranglehold and hooked a hand under the dog's collar, levering himself up. "Trying to make me blow my cover?" he asked, panting. He stroked the dog's head and ruffled his ears, then looked around. He spotted Katie standing a few feet away, gasping for breath. She looked at the two of them and burst into fresh tears.

Griffin's heart twisted. "He's okay, Katie. I just knocked him over. But I didn't hurt him. Really."

"I know that," she sniffled as she wiped her face with her arm. "I'm crying because ... because you caught him in time!"

"Here. Give me his leash." He hooked it on the dog's collar and wrapped it once around his hand. Katie reached over to take the lead, but stopped when Griffin shook his head. "Bear's really juiced up on adrenalin. As big as he is, he could yank you right off your feet if he takes off again. Let me help you walk him home. Okay?"

Katie nodded, wiping her cheeks again. "Yeah. Maybe you're right. He's a big guy, even for a—" She froze as she spotted Griffin's torn shirt, the bloody lines showing through.

"Oh my gosh—you're bleeding!" Katie stepped closer and crouched down, trying to see the damage. "Bear, no! Get back," she scolded as the dog tried to lick her face. "Hold him tight so I can see." She waited until Griffin had manhandled the dog into a sitting position, then leaned over and gingerly pulled up his torn tee shirt, careful not drag the fabric over the scratches. She grimaced as she examined his chest and stomach, touching his skin gently on either side of the wounds.

Griffin stared over her head for a moment, his pulse thundering in his ears, then blinked and took a step back. "I ... I'm okay." He swallowed with difficulty, his mouth dry.

"No, you're not," she said. "Mom's good at first aid. I want her to check your scratches. A couple of them look really deep."

"I'd rather my dad handle it." An embarrassing vision of being shirtless in front of Katie and her mom flashed through his mind. "Let's get Bear and you home first."

Griffin tugged on the dog's leash, but Katie dug in her heels. Grabbing the strap close to Bear's collar, she shook her head, a line appearing between her fair eyebrows. She braced her feet, preventing both dog and boy from moving.

"No way! You want your dad to patch you up? Fine, but we're doing that first. Before we take Bear home."

"Katie, I don't—"

"Griffin, you do," she interrupted him.

"Bossy."

"Stubborn."

They took the long way home, Bear trotting between them.

Basil's Journal: Wednesday, September 18th

Griffin injured himself saving Katie Heflin's ~~horse~~ dog this afternoon. He's quite the knight-in-shining-armor to her now. After I'd promised to take good care of the lad, I sent her and the dog home. Which was a good thing because a little antiseptic ointment on those scratches and he was fussing like a baby. And his favorite shirt was ruined. Even so, he walked around the house all evening grinning and humming to himself.

Methinks a certain someone is In Love.

"Here. Let me hold it for you." Carlee pulled the locker door wider as Katie crouched down, rummaging for her math book on the bottom shelf. "Man, I'm glad tomorrow's Friday! Are you going home or do you wanna go do something?"

"Where's that stupid ... oh, here it is." Katie crammed the textbook into her backpack and yanked the zipper closed. "I need to get home, Carlee. I want to check something out."

"It wouldn't be Griffin, would it? I'd like to check him out, if you know what I mean." Carlee giggled. "You're sure you're not interested in him? Because I don't want to get between you two."

Katie stood up, slinging her bag over one shoulder. The hallway began to empty as the exit-the-building bell clanged over their heads. "Carlee. I ... I kind of like Griffin. And I think he likes me, so ...."

"Say no more. You get first dibs on him. I'm just glad you let me know before I hurt your feelings or anything." Carlee's hazel eyes twinkled. "Promise me you'll keep me informed of any juicy details tomorrow. Okay?" She gave Katie a sudden hug. "Go get him, girlfriend!"

ꟷ

"For the whole weekend?" Katie said again.

"Yeah. He wants to make it a three-day trip," Griffin said. "Get in a training ... I mean, do some camping before winter. We're taking off in a few minutes. I just wanted to ... you know. Make sure Bear didn't get banged up yesterday when I tackled him." He shifted his weight from foot to foot.

"He's fine. I was going to come check on *you*. Do your scratches hurt?"

"Nah, it's all good. They just sting a little." He glanced over his shoulder. "I better go." Licking his lips, he cleared his throat. "Hey, do you want to ... um ... get together next week? Do something?" He crossed his toes inside his shoes.

"Yeah. Yeah, that'd be great!" She grinned. "Call me when you get home. Or just come over."

His heart leaped. He started to speak when a faint whistle made him look around.

"Griffin. Time to go," Basil called from across the street, closing the Saab's hatch with a dull whoosh.

"'Bye, Katie." Griffin smiled, then turned and trotted down the steps, leaping off the last two.

Chapter Seventeen

Katie's Journal: Wednesday, September 25th

MY LIFE IS INSANE! I've got a big project due in science and I have to meet every day after school in the lab with Cas Navarre. Cas is super smart and really fun to work with—I'm glad he and I ended up on the same team. But it means I barely get home before Dad does, then Mom wants us to eat together, then I have a ton of homework, and then they're yelling at me to turn off my light and go to sleep!

Griffin is so lucky to be home-schooled. His life is so mellow compared to mine. No schedule. No pressure to perform. No group members depending on you.

He and his dad were gone all weekend. And now it's already Wednesday night and I haven't seen him all week!

Griffin's Journal: Wednesday, September 25th

Basil just told me we might have some time off starting tomorrow afternoon. Fire, am I ready for a break! Plus I haven't seen Katie since last Wednesday!

We've been on duty around the clock since Sunday night and have already logged twenty-two missions. Four were unsuccessful. Sometimes I envy Katie. Must be nice to just worry about homework and grades and friends and arguing with your parents.

And not worry about people getting hurt or killed if you screw up.

Oh, man, not again! Basil's driving me crazy! He keeps yelling at me to catch a nap before the next call comes in.

I'm getting really tired of sleeping with my shoes on.

ꕥ

"Katie, Griffin's here," called Helen as she ushered him into the living room. "Thank you again for catching Bear last week. It would have broken her heart if anything had happened to him. Are you all right?"

"I'm just glad I could grab him in time—he was really moving!" Griffin scratched the dog under the chin as the huge animal danced in front of him, nails clicking on the wood floor, anxious for the Terrae Angelus' touch. "Those scratches weren't serious. They hurt more when Dad put that ointment on them. He said they won't even scar or anything." He hesitated and took a deep breath. "Would it... would it be okay if Katie and I went to get some coffee? At that new place near the College?"

"Oh-Be-Joyful? That'll be fine. I'll just see what's keeping my daughter. Make yourself at home." Helen nodded toward the sofa and hurried upstairs. She smiled to herself as she reached Katie's room. I know exactly what's keeping my daughter, she thought, and chuckled at the various shirts discarded on the bed as Katie pulled on another tee.

"The blue one looks fine. Wear your denim jacket. Griffin wants to go for coffee—do you need some money? Got your cell? Good. Be back by five-thirty."

ꙮ

Griffin peeked out of the corner of his eye as they strolled along, then glanced down. Should I hold her hand? he thought as he stared at his own in uncertainty. Do I ask first or do I just take it? What if she wants me to and I don't? Or what if I do and she doesn't want me to? And how do humans train for this stuff? Griffin sighed to himself and veered without thinking, taking his regular shortcut through the neighborhood park.

They collided. Katie stumbled, banging her face against Griffin's shoulder. "Ow!" she gasped, holding her nose, her eyes watering. "Oh, crap, that hurts," she said, her voice muffled.

"Katie, I'm sorry! You okay?" Griffin grabbed her arm. "Here, let me see it." He cupped her soft chin in his palm, tilted her head back and examined her face. "It's not bleeding or anything." Letting go, he slid his hand down her arm and squeezed her fingers. "Do you want to go back home?" Please say no, he thought.

She sniffed cautiously, then wiggled her nose. "It's okay now. I've been hurt worse when Bear whacked me with his big ole' head." Grinning, she gripped his hand.

"Good," said Griffin. He threaded his fingers through hers and led the way across the quiet park. I think I'd rather just walk around holding hands then go get coffee, he thought to himself. He smiled as he looked down. Katie peered quizzically at him.

"Your skin's so white compared to mine," he explained. "Are you sure you're not a vampire or something?"

"Yeah. Right," she said, absently glancing around at the empty playground, then her eyes widened. She paused, pulling him to a stop. "Instead of coffee, would you like to—" she spied an oversized tire suspended from chains "—swing?"

He stared at her, then nodded in relief. "You bet. In fact, I—"

"Race you," she shouted as she gave him a shove and sprinted off.

"Hey, that's cheating!" Griffin staggered a step, and then shot after her, legs pumping. Catching up, he slowed and matched her stride, grinning as she jostled him. As they approached the goal, he lunged forward and slapped the tire a split second before her.

"Fire, you're fast! I almost didn't beat you," Griffin gasped. "Notice I said *almost*."

"Well, I let you win. Frail male ego, you know." They both laughed, panting for a moment.

"Okay, I have got to try this thing," said Katie and clambered aboard the enormous tire. As it tilted, she gestured to him. "Get on the other side. That way, we'll balance it."

Grabbing the chains as high as he could reach, Griffin hoisted himself up and over the rim, dangling his legs inside. "Let me get it started," he said. "Hang on." Bending forward, he stretched out a leg, the toe of his athletic shoe brushing the ground. He gave a quick push and the swing began spinning. After he had taken a few more kicks, momentum took over. Hopping back on, Griffin pressed his knees against Katie's, his stomach tingling from the twirling motion. He watched as Katie clasped the chains tightly, then tipped back as far as she could, her hair streaming behind her.

As it slowed down, he kicked again, and this time joined her, leaning out with his eyes shut. Hooking his feet inside the tire rim on either side of her knees, Griffin let go and stretched back, arms spread wide.

Flying.

"Griffin! Be careful!"

"No, it's okay. Just hook your feet inside the rim. Then let go of the chains. It's awesome!"

As she adjusted her seat, he gave the swing an extra hard spin and tilted back again. He laughed for no reason.

Which is always the best reason.

As the tire slowed and then stopped, they both sat up. Grinning, they hopped down inside at the same time. For a long minute, they gazed at each other. Then, bracing his hands on either side of the tire, Griffin leaned forward and half-closed his eyes.

And kissed Katie.

Unsure what to do next, he peeked through slitted eyelids. Spying hers tightly closed, he shut his again. After a few moments, they both drew back, each taking a deep breath.

"I wouldn't mind trying that again," he whispered, "and I don't mean the swing."

Katie laughed nervously, tucking her hair behind one ear, then glanced around the park, checking for spectators. "Okay, I guess," she murmured, then lifted her face and closed her eyes.

They kissed until the shadows chased them home.

Griffin's Journal: Thursday, September 26th

I kissed Katie today.

What was even better: she kissed me back.

Katie's Journal: Thursday, September 26th

I made it home by five-thirty only because Griffin was worried about me being late. He didn't say much, but I have a feeling his dad's pretty strict about him being responsible and all that.

Mom asked me how the coffee shop was. I told her that we hung out at the playground instead. I thought she was going to give me a hard time for changing plans without telling her. *That's why we got you a cell phone, young lady!*

Instead she just smiled at me.

Chapter Eighteen

"KATIE! WAIT UP!" She turned as Nash Baylor called her name. "Headed to lunch?" he asked, smiling and nodding at various people as they made their way through the crowded hall. He relieved her of her heavy pack, carrying both hers and his own with ease—a habit of his for the past week now.

"Yeah. I'm meeting Carlee. How 'bout you?" Katie smiled back.

"I'm eating with the team. We need to go over some strategies. Hey, are you coming to the game tomorrow?" They entered the cafeteria, both grimacing at the slow-moving line.

"I don't think so. Not a big football fan," she said over the clamor of voices. "Anyway, I have to do this family thing Friday night," she quickly added. "But I hope you guys win."

He smiled down at her as they stood waiting for the line to move, his letter jacket emphasizing his large frame. "Me, too! I really want to make it to state this year. Maybe catch the eye of some college scout and all that, even though I'm still a junior. A football scholarship would be amazing."

"Do you know what college you want to go to?"

"I'm thinking about CU and a few others. Have you thought about it yet? Even though you're a sophomore, it's not too early to start planning." Nash groaned, running a hand through his sandy hair. "Crap—I sound just like my dad!" He laughed at himself, Katie joining in.

Still chuckling, she said, "I'll probably go to the College since my dad's a professor there. As long as my scores are high enough, of course." She tucked her hair behind one ear. "I'll live on campus, though."

"Katie! Over here," Carlee called, pointing to the empty chair next to her. Katie nodded and gestured at the long line, then made a face. Carlee flicked her eyes at Nash waving to his teammates on the other end of the cafeteria, then gave a not-so-subtle thumbs up. Katie frowned and shook her head. Carlee snickered.

Nash sighed. "Look, I'm sorry to dump you, but I really need to meet with the guys. You okay in line here?" He hooked her pack over her shoulder.

"I think I can handle it, Nash." She tugged at the strap, settling it more securely. "I've been getting my own lunch tray since kindergarten, you know."

"Just didn't want to be rude or anything," he said. "See you in math, Katie-girl." His hand lingered on her elbow, squeezing it gently as he left.

Katie stood there, watching him, her arm tingling from his touch, then turned to grab a tray. *Katie-girl?* she wondered. What the heck was that all about? She selected a sandwich and orange. Just Nash being Nash, she decided, and hurried over to her friend.

"Girlfriend, you've been holding out on me!" said Carlee before Katie could take a seat. "First Griffin, now Nash? I kind of figured you for a one-boyfriend-at-a-time sort, but I do like your taste. Although, between you and me, Griffin's not even in the same league as Nash."

"Carlee," Katie protested, "I'm not interested in ..."

"For one thing, Griffin's shorter. And he's home-schooled. High geek quotient there. He does have a nice body and a killer smile, but he's no Nash Baylor, if you know what I mean. Plus Nash is older, which gives him ...." Katie stared in amazement as Carlee babbled non-stop until the bell rang.

Katie's Journal: Wednesday, October 11th

I found out that our school is having this big fundraiser on the twenty-seventh (think that's a Friday) called the Harvest Festival. It's to raise money for High Springs' food bank. It's in the gym and you pay to participate in all sorts of games and activities. I thought it sounded lame, but I guess it's a big annual tradition and everyone shows up.

Nash Baylor asked me today in math if I would go with him. I have to admit, he's sweet and totally good-looking, but I told him that I was already planning on bringing someone else. He seemed both mad and surprised. Don't know if he was shocked that I had a boyfriend or that I declined.

I'm sure he doesn't get turned down very often.

I'll feel really stupid if Griffin can't come! He and his dad have the strangest schedule. Sometimes they're around all the time. Sometimes gone for several days. (Weird, because a lot of times Mr. Raine's Saab is in the driveway when I know they're away.) Griffin says it has to do with some project of his dad's and he never knows when they're taking off until they take off. He did tell me that there'll be times he and I have plans and he might not show up. He didn't want me to think he would ever stand me up.

He's so cute when he's worried about messing up. It must be hard for him in some ways. His family life is so different. No mom. Doesn't even have a cell phone. But he doesn't seem to care about stuff like that.

Griffin's Journal: Tuesday, October 17th

Katie asked me to go to a fundraiser at school with her. Some sort of carnival. Sounds fun. She also told me that Nash Baylor, a guy in her math class, asked her, but she turned him down.

Good. He can get his own girlfriend.

Basil said yes, unless we're on call. He even said I could take the car. Made another pathetic joke about my new license. What's with those pictures!!!?? That driver's test was a breeze—I don't see why humans make such a big deal out of turning sixteen. Miss Lena gave me a new MP3 player. I'd rather have a cell phone.

Sixteen. Only two months until the winter solstice.

Basil says there is no way I'm going to fail my Proelium. He told me the test is just another step in the journey. My journey.

But what if I don't pass? What if I become the first Tiro to fail it in like a billion years? How am I supposed to live as a human?

What if Nicopolis was right about me after all?

ϗ

"'*Rule Britannia* ...'" sang Basil under his breath as he checked the lasagna, the aroma of garlic and oregano filling the kitchen. He grated a final dusting of Parmesan cheese over it and artfully arranged a few parsley snips across the top layer, then slid it back into the oven to stay warm. Turning around, he watched as Griffin bustled about, setting the round table for three.

"We so rarely use our dining room to ... well ... dine," said Basil. "It seems like our friends are more comfortable in the kitchen." He reached around his Tiro to adjust the yellow-checked tablecloth.

"Just like Miss Lena," said Griffin, trying to remember which side the forks belonged. "Are they on the left or right?" he asked, holding up several mismatched utensils.

"It depends on which hemisphere you're eating in, I believe," said Basil with a straight face. "It's the opposite in the southern one, you know."

"Right side it is," said Griffin. "The salad's in the fridge. And the garlic bread's ready—I'll warm it up when you serve the lasagna."

The doorbell rang. Before either of them could move, a cheery voice called from the hallway. "Basil, Griffin? Hellooo?"

"WE'RE IN THE KITCHEN," bellowed Griffin. Basil winced, and then reached over and flicked his ear, hard. "Ow! What was that for?" Griffin sputtered, rubbing his head.

At that moment, Lena walked in, fishing in her suit coat pocket. "Oh, thank goodness! I was dreaming of your lasagna all the way here." She inhaled blissfully. "I'm famished." She flung her coat over the back of a chair, keeping an arm hidden behind her. "It has been such a busy week at the Foundation. I barely had time to shop for Griffin."

"Lena," said Basil, stooping down to greet her with a peck. "You're spoiling the lad."

"No, no. Spoil the lad!" Griffin said, sliding around his Mentor to give her a hug. She patted his cheek.

"Hush, both of you," she ordered. "This is the other half of his birthday gift. Now, liebling—I have two stipulations before I give you this."

"*Stipulation*? What's that mean?"

"Conditions, terms, provisions—" Basil began. Griffin pleaded with her silently.

"I want to hear all about your sweetheart," Lena interrupted, her eyes twinkling. She laughed when Griffin blushed, then glared at Basil. "And a photo of Katie would also be lovely."

"How can I ...?" began Griffin, then whooped with delight when Lena whipped her hand around, pressing the new cell phone into his. "Oh, wow! This is awesome! Thanks, Miss Lena!" He flipped it open. "This kind does everything! Look—it takes pictures and downloads and even—"

Lena held up her hand. "I don't care how it works. Do *you* like it? Yes? Then that's all I need to know. Except about Katie, of course. Over dinner, perhaps?"

Chapter Nineteen

Basil's Journal: Friday, October 27th

I OCCASIONALLY REMIND GRIFFIN our training in both agility and team work can be useful other times, not just on missions. Take tonight for example: Griffin was supposed to pick Katie up at six forty-five for a school event. Naturally, we didn't return home from the rescue until six thirty-eight. Both of us filthy from head to toe from the dust and mud of the construction site.

It became Team Angel the instant we bolted through the front door.

Griffin was half undressed by the time his foot hit the first step. Sprinting upstairs, he left a trail of dirty clothing all the way into his bathroom. He had the shower running and was scrubbing down while I scrabbled through his dresser for clean clothes. I wasted precious seconds shouting at him through the bathroom door which sweater he wanted. He hollered for the brown turtleneck. I chose the dark green crew instead. Mentor's prerogative. Threw the sweater and clean jeans on his bed then raced around, frantically trying to locate the car keys. I made it to the front door just as Griffin thundered down the stairs drying his hair. He flung the towel over the newel post and snatched the keys from my hand. I took one swipe at his hair in an attempt to smooth it down. Lost cause.

Front door slammed. I counted to four. Front door hurled open as Griffin snagged his jacket from the hall rack and tore out again.

Six forty-eight.

ꕥ

"I don't think we're going to find a spot any closer than this." Griffin punched off the car's radio, then wheeled into a curbside space next to the downtown square. "We can cut across the park—looks like that's what a lot of people are doing."

"Fine with me," Katie said as she climbed out. "But I think I'll take my jacket. Oh, are you leaving yours?" she asked as he scooted around the car to her side.

"Yeah. Cold doesn't bother me much. Anyway, once we're inside, I'll get too warm from all the people and stuff. No, Katie," he said firmly as she started to toss hers in the back seat. "Bring it with you."

"Now that's a side of you I haven't seen before," she said. "I think I can decide for myself whether I need a coat or not. Anyway, the school's just across the park, for cryin' out loud."

"I promised Dad I'd watch out for you. Promises are a big deal with him and me," he said. He helped her on with her jacket and tugged her collar up around her throat, admiring the way the dark fabric contrasted with her white-blonde hair; he fingered a few strands of it, marveling at its softness. "Angel's wing," he murmured, unaware that he had spoken aloud.

"What?"

"Oh—just talking to myself. Come here, you." He pulled her close. As Katie's fingers played with a damp lock of hair at the back of his neck, Griffin leaned even closer, his hands resting on her slender waist, and kissed her. After a few moments, he broke off and drew back, his brown eyes smoldering in the dim streetlight.

"Guess we should get going," he whispered.

"Guess so," Katie whispered back. They smiled at each other as they locked the car and headed across the park.

ᘓᘐ

"You were right! Looks like your entire school is here," shouted Griffin.

They stood in the double doorway, the roar from the gym vibrating through their feet. Grabbing hands, they joined the crowd, jostling through pockets of people, unsure what to try first. Balls ricocheting off the side of the skeeball ramps vied with the clanging bell on the strongman challenge. Balloons popped with a bang as darts found their targets, while the trampoline in the far corner had a huge audience shouting and cheering for every flip, successful or not. As the crush of students swelled, Griffin tucked Katie behind him, gripping her hand at the small of his back as he led the way, plowing through the room.

Passing the food area, his stomach groaned at the aroma of buttery popcorn and spicy pizza. "Hey, let's get something to eat first—I'm starving!" He stopped in front of a table and ordered an enormous slice of cheese pizza.

"You shouldn't have skipped dinner. I'd have waited for you to at least grab a sandwich or something," she said as they waited. "But it was sweet of you to hurry. Although I'm sorry about my mom. She has this thing about going outside with wet hair. It would've been embarrassing if she had made you go upstairs and dry it or something."

"At least she didn't take a towel to my head. I think she was tempted to." Holding the sagging paper plate in both hands, he headed to the empty bleachers.

Katie grabbed some napkins and followed behind. "Ah, it's a mom thing."

I wouldn't know, Griffin thought. They clambered up a few rows and sat down. "At least we got parents who care about us. Imagine what a lot of kids go through. Some insanely screwed-up people out there." He stared into space as he ate.

"Yeah, I complain about them sometimes, but they're okay—we get along pretty well. Except when Mom and I fight. She can be a control freak. Of course, Dad can be, too." She reached over and peeled some cheese off his pizza, twisting it into a wad before popping it in her mouth. "I feel like I'm behind other girls in getting to go on dates and all that. But, hey!" she brightened. "Here I am. In high school. With a boyfriend. Guess it worked out."

"I'm glad they made you wait. Or you would've had one already and wouldn't have given me a second look," said Griffin gravely. "Plus, things have been kind of rough for Bas ... Dad and me for a couple of years. I hadn't really thought about a girlfriend until I met you." He took another bite.

"Hey, can I ask you something? Why do you start to call your father by his first name? Then catch yourself and say *Dad*? I notice you do that a lot."

Griffin stuffed the last of the pizza into his mouth and swallowed, stalling. He wiped his lips with a napkin, then balled it up and tossed it into a nearby trashcan. Sighing, he looked down at his feet, jiggling a leg until he reached a decision.

"Can I tell you something? Something really important?" he asked. Katie laid her hand over his and squeezed it.

Okay, he thought. Here goes nothing. Griffin cleared his throat. "Basil's not ... um ... my real dad. He's like a foster father, but more. Like being adopted, but not quite. We've been together for almost three years now. The best years of my life. Basil, *Dad*, decided it would be less complicated if we just went with the whole father-son routine. He's like a dad in every way. Except that one way. Does that make sense?" He kept his eyes focused on the gym floor, afraid to look up.

"Did you lose your family ... or ...?" Her voice trailed off.

"No, I was with ... I was with ...." He stopped and swallowed, embarrassed at the sudden lump in his throat. "I was with another mentor, you might say. He was ... I mean, he used to ...." Griffin paused and glanced over at her. "It was bad. Really bad."

Katie blinked back tears, unable to speak. She raised her hand and touched the scar near his lower lip, her eyes asking the question. He nodded once and looked down.

"I was so messed up when I came to live with Basil. I don't know how we made it through those first few months. Mostly because he wouldn't give up on me. He made me feel like I was worth something. Worth his time and energy." Griffin shook his head in amazement.

"He saved me, Katie."

She swiped at the tears rolling down her face, then threw an arm over Griffin's shoulders and pulled his head next to hers.

"If I ever meet that guy," she whispered, "I'm ...I'm siccing Bear on him."

Griffin chuckled, his eyes shiny. "Or else Bear could just sit on him and slobber 'em to death. Your dog's breath is toxic!" He gave her a grateful hug, then ran a hand across his face. Standing up, he grabbed her elbow and helped her down the bleachers. "Enough of this emo crap. Let's go try some games. There's an incredibly ugly stuffed animal that I need to win for you!" Laughing, they dove into the crowd.

ꟸ)(ꟹ

Katie's mouth hung open in astonishment; the other students clustered around, watching as the teacher scrambled to set up a second gameboard. He handed Griffin another couple of darts, waving off the teen's money for the next round and nodded at the balloons.

Gripping a dart in each hand, Griffin shifted his weight, balancing on the balls of his feet. He raised his arms and focused on the balloons arranged in a random pattern on the wooden backstop. After a brief pause he let fly. A sharp bang followed as two of the targets popped simultaneously, the darts buried deep. Shouts for a repeat performance echoed around the gym. As more students rushed over, the teacher blew up additional balloons, his face red with exertion.

"Hey, Katie! What's going on?" She turned her head as Nash Baylor appeared behind her, several of his teammates nearby.

"Watch this—it's unreal! Griffin can hit two balloons."

Nash scoffed. "So that's your boyfriend, huh? Heck, anyone with a decent eye and mediocre pitching skills can do that. What's the big deal?"

"Really? At one time?"

Nash frowned as he studied the layout of the game board. "No way he can do that. The first ones were a fluke, that's all. This is a waste—let's go try the trampoline." Nash took Katie's elbow and began to steer her away. His teammates followed.

She jerked her arm free. "Let go, Nash! I'm here with Griffin and I want to watch him. Do you mind?"

Nash's face reddened when his buddies snickered. He glared over her head at Griffin, then down at Katie. Spinning on his heels, he stormed away, shoving past Carlee as she joined her friend, a spool of cotton candy in one hand.

"What was Nash all pissed about?" Carlee tugged a wisp free and licked it off her fingers. "Did I miss Griffin's next attempt? The line was super long, but I'm crazy for cotton candy. I know it's pure sugar, but it's so good! This Festival is a blast. I hear Centennial's been doing it for years. One of the teachers told us today in class ...." Katie smiled absently at her chattering friend while she focused on Griffin conferring with the teacher.

Coming to some agreement with Griffin, the teacher picked up the board, shooed students aside, and moved it a further ten feet away. He braced it against two chairs, then hustled over and handed Griffin eight darts. A low buzz filled the gym as those in the back demanded to know what was happening.

Griffin faced the target, arms by his side, his eyes half closed, lips parted. The sudden blur of movement startled the crowd as all eight balloons exploded. Silence filled the gym for a moment, until the board toppled forward and landed face down, snapping the darts in half.

The audience roared. After a round of high fives and pats on the back, people began drifting away to other activities. Griffin turned around, craning his neck as he searched for a glint of blonde hair. He smiled in relief when he spotted her plowing through the crowd, Carlee in tow. Katie beamed at him as she held up a turquoise crocodile and a black and pink polka dot rabbit in triumph. She rushed over and thrust both creatures into his arms.

"He let me pick the prizes. Technically, you really should have three, but that seemed like overkill," Katie said. "I know you won them for me, but you should take one, too."

Griffin shuddered. "No way! They'll give me nightmares." Carlee, standing nearby, her lips purple from the cotton candy, snickered.

They looked up as the lights flickered on and off, signaling the end of the Festival. Shouts for five more minutes filled the gym. Teachers shook their heads, pointed at the clock, and began ushering students outside.

"I better get going," Carlee said, digging through her purse for her car keys. "If I go an entire month without getting grounded, Mom's letting me have a Christmas party."

"Where are you parked, Carlee?" asked Griffin.

"In the gym lot. Right outside the side door." Finding her keys, she dashed away, yelling for Katie to call her tomorrow.

They turned, squeezing into the pack funneling through the double doors, Griffin leading the way. He staggered as the crowd battered him, tearing Katie's hand loose from his. Pinned to one side by the mob, he peered around, trying to spot her. "Katie?" he called over the buzz of voices.

An elbow rammed into his ribs, slamming him against the cinder-block wall. A second blow to the same spot bent him double. Breathless with pain, he looked up.

"Oh. Sorry. My arm slipped," said Nash Baylor with a sneer. His buddies clustered about, forming a screen and hiding Nash and Griffin from the teachers on duty.

"What's your problem?" wheezed Griffin. He forced himself to stand up straight.

"You." Nash rested a hand against the wall next to Griffin's head as he leaned closer. "You think you're so cool just because you're dating Heflin and can throw some darts."

"Oh, I don't think I'm *cool*," Griffin said, pasting a cocky smile on his face and refusing to back down. "I think I'm *awesome*." He braced himself, ready for the attack.

"Boys! Break it up and get outside," yelled one of the coaches from the doorway. "I want to go home, too, you know." Nash and the others looked around, and then sauntered off, one of them shoving Griffin with his shoulder as they left, pushing through the crowd.

Bunch of jerks, he thought, leaning against the wall and rubbing his side. Fire, I so could have taken him. Heck, all of them! A little Might with my punch and they'd be crying for their mommas. He snorted. And then Basil would kill me for getting in a fight and using my powers. His head whipped around at the sound of Katie's voice.

"Griffin! I've been looking everywhere for you outside," she grumbled as she appeared, her nose pink with the cold. "What are you still doing in here?"

Getting my butt kicked around, he thought to himself. "Nothing. Got stuck in the back. Sorry you had to wait." He took the toys from her and tucked them under his arm. "Come on, let's get out of here."

They hurried across the park. Katie was shivering by the time they reached the car. "Now I'm glad you made me bring my jacket. I'm freezing!" she complained as Griffin helped her in. "I wish I had my gloves."

"Hang on. I'll get the heater going." He shut her door and dashed around to the driver's side, pausing to toss the stuffed animals in the backseat. After turning on the engine, he flipped the heater to the highest setting.

She rubbed her hands briskly and held them in front of the vent. "I can't seem to get warm."

"I think I can help with that," he said. Twisting to face her, he reached over and clasped Katie's hands, turning her sideways in her seat. Holding tight, he pulled her hands nearer and tucked them up under his sweater, pressing them against his tee shirt with a slight flinch. "Warmer?" he asked, after a minute.

Katie sighed, relaxing. "Much." Sliding her hands gently across his ribs, she gazed into his eyes and smiled as his heart began hammering under her right palm, the vibrations running up her arm. Griffin let go of her and spread his arms wide, resting one on top of the steering wheel, and draping the other over the headrest. He held his breath as Katie leaned forward and kissed him.

After a moment, she said, "Your heart's pounding like crazy!"

"Yeah?" said Griffin in a shaky voice. "Well, it always does whenever a girl kisses me."

Katie reared back, jerking her hands free. "And just how many are we talking about here?"

"Oh, you know. All my other girlfriends," he teased, breaking the tension. Pushing his hair off his forehead, he checked the dashboard clock, remembering the previous week when Mr. Heflin had taken him aside for a firm talk about appropriate behavior. More like a lecture than a talk. Fire, what is it with fathers? First Basil, then Mr. Heflin! I mean, where's the trust? He shook his head as he tugged his sweater into place.

"We better go. I shouldn't be idling the car this long, and you've got curfew in twenty minutes." He buckled in and turned on the radio, then smiled. "Oh, good tune!"

"You're kidding," said Katie as she clicked her seatbelt. "Ring of Fire?"

"What? You got something against Johnny Cash?" asked Griffin as he checked the mirror, then pulled away from curb, humming under his breath.

ഇഗ

"You're home early. Everything all right?" called Basil as Griffin shut the door and hung up his jacket.

Stepping across the hallway into the study, Griffin grinned at the sight of his tall Mentor stretched out, stockinged feet hanging off the arm of the sofa and latest novel in hand. "Why didn't you get a longer couch?" he asked.

"It wouldn't fit in the room. And you're evading my question."

"Oh. It was okay," he said with a shrug. "I won a couple of prizes for Katie, but I wanted to get her home before curfew."

"Trying to score points with Father Lewis?" Basil chuckled at Griffin's fervent nod. "Always a good strategy, Tiro. By the way, we're back on standby, so it was fortunate you came home when you did."

Griffin grunted in acknowledgement, then walked around the desk and threw himself into the chair, rolling it back and forth a few times, its wheels squeaking.

"Basil?"

"Fin."

"How do you know if you love someone or just like them a lot?"

Here we go, Basil thought to himself. Closing the book and tossing it on the coffee table, he swung his legs around and sat up. "That is an age-old question, Griffin. And I don't believe there's a simple answer." He leaned back, and clasped his hands behind his head. "It's probably even more complex for us, since our concept of love is somewhat different from the human concept. However, love in its purest form knows no species, age, gender, geography, politics, or religion. Love is simply love. Philosophers and great spiritual leaders have often ..."

He stopped when the beam of Light stabbed the room. They jumped to their feet, listening intently to the quiet voice within it. "Right. On our way," said Basil, and then bent over to thrust his feet into his boots as the brightness faded. Griffin grabbed both their jackets from the hallway hooks and opened the door. They shot outside, raced to the edge of the porch and disappeared into the air, the door banging closed behind them. The scent of a meadow in the sunlight lingered for a moment, and then faded.

Chapter Twenty

Basil gasped for air as he broke the surface of the pond a second time, the little boy cradled against his chest coughing feebly and dribbling water down his tiny chin. Swimming one-handed to the bank, he heaved the child up into Griffin's waiting arms. "How's the girl?" he panted as he trod water, his breath forming a halo around his head.

"She hacked up a gallon. Cold and getting colder," Griffin shouted over the wind as he hoisted the boy higher in his arms, patting the small back as he prepared to clamber up the steep slope.

"I'm going after the father," called Basil. "There's still time."

"Do you want me to try?"

"No! You keep those children from hypothermia. Do whatever it takes!"

Sucking in a deep breath, Basil turned and dove for the submerged car, churning the water behind him with powerful kicks, the seconds ticking in his head. I still have time, he thought as he swam into the inky depths. The man has only been under a few minutes. This freezing water will slow his heart and brain functions. I still have time. Reaching the car, Basil yanked the driver's door off its hinges with a surge of Might, and then ripped the seatbelt in half. A child's sweater floated past him, waving a sleeve.

As he struggled to free the man's legs trapped under the dashboard, the car shuddered, then jerked from side to side. He stopped, peering through the murk in confusion as the wreck began rising, slowly at first, then more rapidly. *Oh, clever lad!* Bracing himself in the open door frame, Basil rose with the car, his white head breaking the surface first, followed by the roof, than the rest of the vehicle. Water sluiced off as a mound of earth lifted them clear. Basil stepped back, sinking slightly in the mud. Crouching down by the half-drowned victim, he placed both hands on either side of the man's ribs and concentrated. He nodded in relief as water gushed out of the man's mouth; after a few moments, the man opened his eyes.

"My kids!" he rasped, his head lolling to one side. "Where...?"

"Your children are fine. Just rest for a minute. The paramedics are on their way." I must remember to thank Lena again for Griffin's cell phone, he thought. Mine is now waterlogged. Fortunately, he had his along. Speaking of which....

"Fin!" Basil shouted up at the figures silhouetted against a flickering glow. "Brilliant solution—raising the car. Why didn't I think of that?" He waited, frowning at the silence. After checking on the man once more, he leaped toward the bank and waded ashore.

"Griffin?" he called again. He gave a sharp whistle, cocking his head, and then scrambled up the side. The scream of the rescue trucks grew louder as he reached the crest and sprinted toward the trio.

Griffin sat cross-legged on the ground in front of a small fire, head drooping, both children warm and sleepy against his chest, wrapped in his jacket. Basil skidded to a halt next to him and dropped to his knees. He grimaced at the sight of Griffin shivering uncontrollably and his lips turning blue with cold.

"What the bloody heck did you do?"

"Izz evvy un 'kay?" Griffin slurred, his mouth and jaw stiff. He fought to open his eyes.

"Yes. Except you. You fool—tried to do too much, didn't you?"

Griffin blinked, unable to focus. "Wurr, dinnid?"

At that moment, the trucks came screeching to a halt. Firemen leaped out, shouting directions as they prepared to lower the stretcher to the car parked on a muddy island in the middle of the pond. The ambulance's doors crashed open. Grabbing their bags, the paramedics rushed over to the little boy and girl waiting alone and forlorn on the bank, shivering as they gazed up into an empty sky.

A jacket lay discarded next to a dying heap of coals.

ꕥ

"How many times do I have to tell you?" said Basil, hauling a semi-conscious Griffin through the front door. "One Element at a time! You're not old enough to handle two yet." Griffin responded by collapsing in the hallway. Basil caught him just before he hit the floor. He hooked an arm behind Griffin's legs and leaned him back, scooping him up with a grunt.

"Puh ee down. M'too big." Griffin flapped his dangling arm in protest as his head lolled against his Mentor's shoulder.

"Stuff and nonsense! Why, one of the requirements of being a Mentor is the ability to lug about your idiotic Tiros when they damage themselves." Basil hoisted him more securely in his arms, then climbed heavily up the stairs to Griffin's bedroom. Kicking the door open, he edged in sideways and lowered the shivering youth onto the bed, stripping the quilt out from under him. He tugged off Griffin's shoes and tucked him in under the cover, pulling it up to his chin. He grabbed a thick comforter from the closet and added it to the mound, then took a seat on the edge of the bed.

"There's more bedding than angel," he said, relieved to see a faint smile through Griffin's chattering teeth. "Let's not do that again, eh?"

"Ya jez dun wahna do m'chores."

"Certainly not. One of the benefits of having an apprentice is the free labor," Basil said as he stood up. "I'll make you some hot tea. Do you want anything else?"

"Zox? Ma feeter c-cold."

"Better yet, I'll bring you a hot water bottle. Old-fashioned, but it does the trick. Back in a jiffy."

Griffin gazed bleary-eyed at the ceiling, listening to the distant bangs and rattles of Basil rummaging around the kitchen. He shivered and snuggled deeper under the comforter. *I wish I could use both Elements at the same time without getting wasted,* he thought. *Basil makes it look so easy. Guess he's right—I gotta be older.* A grin crept across his face. *Still, he told me to do whatever it took to keep those kids warm. So I did.* He sighed and rolled over, curling on his side. *I'm glad we could rescue that family. It was a good thing I came home early from my date with Katie.*

"Katie," he murmured, his smile widening as he replayed their kiss in the Saab. He burrowed deeper into his pillow and closed his eyes. Sleep flowed over him, pressing him down and lifting him up.

Katie's Journal: Sunday, October 29th

What a boring weekend! Cold and cloudy both days. Griffin's still sick. Mr. Raine told me he has to stay in bed. I KNEW he should have worn his jacket to the Festival! My stuffed animals looked great in my room for about six hours until Bear got a hold of them. Mom's pissed because there are pieces all over the house. I can't find the eyes off the crocodile. I think Bear ate them.

My cell's ringing...

Griffin's Journal: Sunday, October 29th

Finally feeling better. I wanted to call Katie yesterday but I felt too lousy to do anything but sleep. Good thing we heal a lot faster than humans. I remember when I was fourteen and broke my arm in two places. I think I only had to wear a cast for six days!

I wonder where my jacket is? Basil's going to go ballistic when I tell him I lost another one. I'm glad I keep my phone in my jeans!

When I called Katie this afternoon, I told her to go look out her bedroom window and wave at me. She said she would show me how to text so we can communicate while sitting at our windows. I suggested we could just walk across the street and she accused me of being too down to earth!!

Of course, Katie being Katie, she had to tease me about getting sick. Said it was because I left my jacket in the car.

I wish I could tell her the truth ....

Chapter Twenty-One

Basil's Journal: Monday, November 13th

THE HEFLINS INVITED US for the upcoming Thanksgiving dinner. Helen informed me her mother was staying in Iowa with her brother's family this year and they would love to have us. Especially since Fin and Katie are inseparable. I have to admit: I enjoy Lewis and Helen's company. Salt of the earth, those two.

However, I'm beginning to feel ... apprehensive ... about the lovebirds. A few of my other Tiros dated humans, several of them quite seriously, but they were older and understood the ramifications. I don't think our lad's that sophisticated.

Curious. There appears to be two Griffins.

One Griffin is such a capable Terrae Angelus. He can quickly analyze a critical situation and has come up with some brilliant solutions. He's helped or saved so many mortals in the last three years. Never once complained about injuries or exhaustion, and even had the foresight to explain to Katie that there might be times he'd fail to show up for a date. All very mature behavior.

Then there's the other Griffin. The one that's truly interacting for the first time with beings his own age (so to speak). When I observe him with Katie, he seems so ... human. Exploring the part of his nature that's more Terrae than Angelus. Learning the nuances of human society. As his fondness for her grows, there's a part of him that wants to share his true nature with her. There's a bigger part of him that knows why he can't.

I tried to talk with him about the possibility that Katie may reject him if she ever found out. He dismissed the idea with a joke.

That's because he's never experienced that heartbreak before. I pray he never does.

ᘓᘐ

"Bear! No! Out of the kitchen, you Clydesdale!" Lewis scurried to rescue the platter of salmon from under the dog's nose and slid it further back on the counter. "Kathleen Heflin! Come subdue your beast!"

"I'll get him." Griffin hurried in from the den and grabbed Bear's collar. "Come on, big guy. It's prison for you." He hauled the wolfhound over to his enormous kennel at one end of the Heflin's kitchen.

Basil worked at the nearby table, ruthlessly whipping sweet potatoes into fluffy mounds. The aroma of turkey and stuffing and yeast rolls rising filled the large kitchen, the rare overcast day contrasting with the warmth and light of the Heflin home.

Glancing over as Griffin wrestled the unwilling dog into the cage, Basil harrumphed. "Now why didn't I think of that? It would have been ideal for Fin when he was younger," he said. "A couple of chew toys, a tattered blanket, and Bob's your uncle."

"It's not too late, you know," said Lewis over his shoulder as he sliced the fish into precise fillets.

"Hey!" protested Griffin.

They both laughed, then Lewis asked. "By the way, where *is* my daughter?"

"Mrs. Lewis and her went—" began Griffin, only to be interrupted.

"Mrs. Lewis and she ...." corrected Basil.

"*Mrs. Lewis and she*—" exaggerated Griffin, "—went to the store to get more whipped cream."

"Bear?" guessed Lewis.

"Oh, yeah! Katie said that he might need to go outside sooner than later." Griffin studied the restless dog. "Oops! Better make that *now*!" Yanking open the kennel, he grabbed Bear's collar and guided him to the back door. He snagged his jacket off the chair as he pushed the dog out ahead of him and quickly shut the door against the chilly air.

Lewis peered out the kitchen window. "He's a good kid, Basil," he said. "You've done a fine job with him."

"Why, thank you, Lewis. As did you and Helen with your young miss."

"I ... um ... Katie told me about your situation. The fostering," said Lewis, careful to keep his eyes on the task in hand.

"Yes. Well. My apologies for being less than forthcoming earlier. I wasn't sure how you would react," said Basil. "Some people have preconceived notions about foster children."

"I don't blame you. I mean, you hardly knew us, and you were protecting Griffin." He cleared his throat. "Katie mentioned he had said his previous fostering was ... rough."

"Rough doesn't begin to describe it. If you had known Fin three years ago, it would have broken your heart." Basil absentmindedly beat the potatoes into a soup, the whisk clanging rhythmically as he stared into space. "He was so guarded, Lewis. It was months before he really trusted me." He stopped and looked down, lost in memories. "I was fortunate he finally opened up. So I could help him."

Lewis smiled gently. "I think Griffin was the fortunate one."

ꝏ

Flinching from another attack on his anklebone, Griffin kicked back at Katie in retaliation; he missed, striking the table leg instead. Katie giggled and tucked her foot further under her chair, her eyes on her plate as she choked silently with laughter.

"Okay, you two. That's enough!" said Helen. "Quit playing footsie and eat your dinner." She sighed and appealed to her husband for support as the table shuddered again, causing china and silver to jangle. Before Lewis could step in, Basil took charge.

Still chewing, he reached over and snagged Griffin's ear with one hand, then smiled at the adults as he continued eating, increasing the pressure with his thumb and forefinger. He gave it a twist for good measure.

"Ow!" Griffin winced. "Okay, okay, I get the message."

Basil swallowed. "Loud and clear?" he asked before taking another bite, enjoying his meal as well as Lewis' and Helen's grins and Katie's mortification. He pinched harder.

"Very clear." His eyes watering, Griffin tried to pull away. No such luck.

Basil chewed and swallowed again. "Do I need to finish this delicious dinner one-handed?"

"No, sir," gasped Griffin.

"Are you sure?"

"Yes, sir!"

Releasing the youth's ear, now a shade redder, he continued eating, then inclined his head as Helen and Lewis raised their glasses in a salute. Griffin massaged his ear and exchanged embarrassed glances with Katie.

"Oh, I was going to ask you, Helen—where did you get the angel statue by the front steps? It's quite striking," said Basil.

"Why, thank you. It took longer than I'd planned to have it shipped from Iowa," she said. "I'm trying to find the perfect poem or quotation to have engraved on its base." She leaned back and took a sip of wine, her fingernail flicking the edge of the glass with a musical ping. "We discovered it in an antique shop outside Oxford when Lewis was doing some research there. The summer before Katie was born."

"Oxford—that's your old stomping grounds, isn't it?" asked Lewis.

"You might say." Basil buttered his roll. "What were you researching? Katie, the cranberry sauce, if you don't mind."

The professor laughed, a little self-conscious. "It's an obscure fable in angelic lore, really, although traces of it are found in Judaism, Islam, and Christianity, as well as in many other religions." Resting his elbows on the table, he steepled his fingers and launched into instructor mode. "According to this legend, there's a type of guardian angel that lives here on Earth. Supposedly they're so much like us we can't tell them apart from humans. Outside of some vague references, the only source we really have is a medieval document called the Kellsfarne manuscript."

As Lewis talked, Basil sat frozen, a fixed smile on his face. He stole a glance at Griffin and gave a slight shake of his head as the professor continued.

"It was written in the twelfth century by an abbot, Aidan, who was head of the Kellsfarne monastery. How he learned of these ...." He stopped when Griffin began coughing.

"You okay?" he asked.

Griffin took a sip of water, nodding his head. "Swallowed wrong," he rasped, then took a deeper drink.

"So do these ... angels ... have a name?" asked Basil. Griffin held his breath.

"*Terrae Angeli.* The translation into English would be *earth angels,* I believe. My Latin's a bit rusty," admitted Lewis. "Goodness! Listen to me ramble on. Probably just one of those quirky stories that only dusty old scholars like me care about."

"What if it's true?" Griffin ignored the look his Mentor gave him.

"You mean, angels and all that?" asked Katie.

"Well, sure. A lot of people believe in celestial angels. Why not another kind? That help people directly. Here on earth." Griffin stared at Katie before turning to Lewis. "You said they were a kind of *guardian* angel, didn't you?"

"Griffin—" began Basil. Lewis interrupted him with a wave of his hand.

"Oh, I don't mind answering his questions," Lewis assured him, mistaking Basil's tone. "Griffin, angels can be found in most world religions and are often thought of as benevolent beings that serve God and aid humankind. However, some religions also believe that angels have free will. So they're capable of both great good and great evil. Many people find that idea ... disturbing." He smiled at Griffin's expression. "Personally, I'm not sure if I believe in supernatural beings or not."

"Well, I don't. I think things just happen," said Katie.

Helen snorted at her. "My pragmatic daughter." She shook her head and then glanced around the table. "I *do* think angels are out there. Watching over us. We just don't know it." She sighed and added softly, "I would love to meet one. Just once."

Griffin started to speak, but stopped when Basil nudged his knee under the table. Nodding reluctantly, he dropped the subject.

ꙮ

Katie and Griffin strolled down the street toward the park, both of them holding Bear's leash as he trotted ahead, his rough coat the same color and texture as the snow-heavy clouds. She paused and handed the lead to Griffin, then tucked a few stray hairs under her blue cap, tugging it down lower over her ears.

"Thanks, let me take him. Now watch this—I've been doing some training," she said, grasping the leash in her gloved hand. "Bear. Heel," she ordered. She staggered as the giant lunged forward, dragging her down the street.

"How's that working for you?" called Griffin as he jogged behind her. He caught up as they turned into the park. Grabbing her hand, he tugged her toward the tire swing.

She stared with disbelief. "And I thought you wanted to walk off all that turkey. So you could have room for pie."

"I did." He grinned, his eyes twinkling. "But since we're here, I thought we might ... you know ... *swing*. Tie Bear over there to that post."

Katie dragged the dog across the play area and looped the leash around a rung on the monkey bars as Griffin hurried over to the tire swing and clambered onboard. She joined him, waiting for him to push off. Instead, he jumped inside, pulling her down with him. Wrapping his arms around her waist, he leaned in for a kiss.

"Listen," she said, pushing him away with a grin. "I like kissing as well as the next person, but I'm freezing!" She straightened her cap and zipped her jacket higher under her chin.

"Cold, eh? I'll warm you up," he said, trying to steal another kiss. Giggling, she slithered out of his arms and ducked out from under the tire. She squealed with laughter when he leaped up on the rim and gave a mock howl, then jumped, pretending to pounce on her.

Bear went berserk.

The dog roared, rearing from side to side before ripping the leash loose, frantic to defend Katie. Tearing across the playground at a dead run toward them, he bellowed his war cry, his lips peeled back from his fangs and his hackles stiffened in rage. With a snarl, he launched himself at her assailant.

Without thinking, Griffin flung out both hands, fingers spread wide.

Bear plowed muzzle-first into the gravel, yelping as he rolled over twice from the force of the Terrae Angelus' Might. Scrambling to his feet, the dog shook his head and whined, the fight knocked out of him. A few specks of blood beaded his gray-brown nose. Belly low to the ground, he crept over to them.

"By the Light!" Griffin said unevenly. He held a hand out for the dog to sniff. "Stupid goof—you scared the crap out of me!" At Bear's apologetic lick, he thumped the dog's ribs good-naturally and glanced over at Katie. "What the heck was that about?"

"I-I guess he thought you were attacking me," she explained, her face pale. "Man, I thought he was going to tear into you or something! We're lucky he tripped."

"Real lucky," he said vaguely. He frowned as he studied her. "Hey, are you all right?"

"Oh, yeah. No problem. Nothing like your dog trying to eat your boyfriend to really warm up a person." She chuckled weakly. "But I think I want to go home now."

As they headed back, hand in hand and Bear slinking along next to Katie, Griffin cleared his throat. "Katie? Did you really mean it? At dinner when you said you didn't believe in ... um ... angels?"

"What?"

"Angels. You don't think they might actually exist?"

"Well, no. No, I don't," she said. "Why? Do you?"

He shrugged. "Why not?"

Katie peered up at Griffin, searching his face. "You're kidding, right? How can you believe in ... in ... in people in nightgowns with fluffy wings? Flying around playing harps? Wearing halos?" She snorted. "Just saying it sounds stupid."

He halted, dropping her hand. "It's not stupid. And *that* image of angels is something people made up to sell Christmas cards or whatever." He spread his arms wide. "What if angels, guardian angels like the Terrae Angeli, really do exist? Like every time something happens that's fortunate for a person, it's really an angel helping them?"

Katie shook her head. "This is a ridiculous conversation. Who gives a rip if they exist or not? As long as they stay away from me. A guardian angel reminds me of a creepy stalker." She snickered at her own joke.

Griffin froze, surprised at his pain. He opened and closed his mouth, then looked away. "Is that what you really think?" he asked stiffly.

"Yeah, that's what I really think." Katie frowned in confusion. "Griffin, what's going on?" Her eyes opened wide as he clenched his jaw and turned his back on her, his hands shoved deep in his pockets. "Griffin?"

Without another word, he walked away.

ꕥ

Unable to sleep, Griffin sat cross-legged on his bed, his elbows propped on his knees and his chin cupped in his hands as he gazed out at Katie's dark window. As he watched, the snow began—big, heavy, wet flakes, covering lawns and rooftops, cars and streets, blanketing all things equally. The city's lights reflected off the cloud cover, casting an unearthly glow across High Springs.

His thoughts swirled like the growing storm. What if I told her? What if she finally knew what I was? Would it change her mind about angels? Or would she just think I was some kind of freak? Would she be scared of me? Would she be angry because I lied to her? In a way?

Would she hate me?

Chapter Twenty-Two

Katie's Journal: Thursday, November 24th

ALL I SAID IS THAT I DON'T BELIEVE in angels and he got pissed! And just walked off! If he wants to believe in them, fine. Just count me out. He sure seemed to take it personally. Maybe I shouldn't have laughed at him. Dad's always telling me you have to be careful not to offend other people's beliefs.

If you ask me, it seems a little weird that a guy would be that much into angels. I mean, Griffin's a lot different from other boys, but come on!

This has got to be the worst Thanksgiving ever!

Griffin's Journal: Friday, November 25th

My girlfriend doesn't believe in ... well ... *me*. And I have my Proclium coming up. Gosh, no pressure there— just my ENTIRE FUTURE DEPENDING ON WHETHER I PASS OR NOT!!!

Could my life suck any more?

Griffin's Journal: Friday, November 25th (cont.)

Apparently, it can.

Basil just found out that there might be a possibility that Nicopolis may be the Senior Mentor overseeing my test.

I'm freaked. He's angry.

Basil's going to meet with Command to see if I can have another Mentor. He seems pretty sure he can get another one assigned. Especially since we had that meeting with Guardian Mayla.

I still remember every detail about that day. I think she believed me, but the rest of Command? Who knows? Basil told me that when it comes down to believing a Mentor and believing a Tiro, Command will almost always choose the Mentor.

He also said life was unfair that way.

You think?

Katie's Journal: Friday, November 25th

It's only been one day and I miss Griffin. Angel obsession and all.

Griffin's Journal: Saturday, November 26th

I want to call Katie, but I don't want to call her. But I miss her.

What *do* humans believe, anyway? Mrs. Lewis said she did. Mr. Lewis said he wasn't sure. Katie thinks...well, I know what she thinks. Is that how it is with the others? Some do. Some don't. The rest are unsure?

Screw all this! I'm phoning Katie. She should be up by now.

ꕥ

"Sorry again about the fight," said Griffin, squeezing Katie's hand as they walked through the neighborhood toward downtown, the sky a sapphire bowl overhead.

"You already told me that. And I'm sorry, too. So it's all okay. Okay?" Katie shook her head as she unzipped her jacket. "I can't believe the snow's already melted," she said, changing the subject. "I thought Colorado would have snow all winter, but there's barely any left. Just under the trees and—"

"Hush!" Griffin pulled her to a stop, head cocked to one side as he scanned the street. "Thought I heard something."

Katie frowned. "Like what?"

"Like a heavy crash and then someone ... " They whipped their heads around as a woman screamed from several houses away.

"Oh, God! I need help! My husband ... Someone help me!"

Griffin dropped Katie's hand and sprinted down the street toward the sound. Pounding up the driveway, he skidded to a halt as a hysterical woman stumbled out of an open garage.

"The car fell on my husband!" She grabbed his arm, pulling at him frantically. "I can't get it off of him!"

Griffin shook free and rushed inside, sliding to his knees beside the vehicle. A pair of legs poked out from underneath the car, which was tilted to one side, with a wheel missing. A jack lay nearby. Griffin glanced around, then nodded to himself. Turning his head, he spotted Katie standing next to the sobbing woman in the driveway.

"Katie," he called. "You two stay outside. Understand?" The girl nodded, her face white. "It'll be okay," he added. "But stay out there."

He turned back and shuffled forward on his knees, edging closer as the man groaned faintly. "Hang on, sir. Help's coming," he said. Taking a deep breath, he leaned over, placed both palms against the garage floor and grunted as he pushed down. Cracks radiated from his hands. The concrete buckled like an accordion and lifted the car off the man. Lying flat on his stomach, Griffin wriggled underneath the car. Good, he's breathing, he thought, laying his hand on the man's chest. He retreated, then grabbing the man by the shoulders, dragged him carefully over the broken concrete and across the oil-stained floor.

"Hank!" shouted the woman, pulling free of the girl's grip. She rushed into the garage and knelt beside her groaning husband. "Hank! Oh, please let him be okay!" She shook him gently.

Griffin took her cold hands, holding them between his warm ones. "Ma'am, you don't want to move him right now. He's breathing, so that's good." The woman nodded, her eyes fixed on her husband's face. "We'll stay with you until the ambulance gets here." He looked around for Katie, then smiled when he saw her already talking on her phone, stepping around to the front of the house for the address. "Good girl," he whispered.

The woman sniffed as she looked at Griffin, then at the car listing to one side. "How did you do that?" she asked tearfully.

"The floor must have been cracked already. The car made it buckle even further when it fell," Griffin explained. "What was he doing, anyway?" he asked, changing the subject.

"Just working on it. I ... I don't know." Biting her lip, she wiped the tears still running down her face, then clasped her husband's hand and visibly settled herself to wait. After a few minutes, they both brightened at the sirens' screams.

As the ambulance and fire truck coasted to the curb and uniformed men began leaping to the ground, Griffin rose to his feet and slipped outside. Oh, crap, he thought, staring at the rescue vehicles. Not those guys again! Joining the neighbors lining the driveway, he knelt down, pretending to tie his shoe. Keeping his head bowed, he waited until the paramedics rushed past him, then jumped up. "Come on, Katie," he said, grabbing her hand and pulling her through the crowd and down the street.

She looked back over her shoulder. "Don't we need to stay and ... and ... fill out a form or something?"

"Nah. They'll take it from here." Picking up the pace, he hustled her around the corner, then stopped and sank down on a low wall, his pulse racing. Katie sat down next to him. She snuggled in as he wrapped an arm around her shoulder. For several minutes, they sat holding each other, Katie trembling.

She winced at the wail of the ambulance as it raced past the end of the street and burrowed closer to Griffin. "Wow, that was scary. I can't stop shaking."

He rubbed her arm briskly, then leaned over and kissed the top of her head. "You did good. Thanks for calling 911 and not freaking out or anything."

Laughing with relief, she peeked up at his face. "I'm surprised I remembered the number! And how come you're so calm?"

Griffin held out a shaky hand. "Not so much."

They smiled at each other, the sun shining on their faces and the stone wall warm beneath them. Then Griffin pulled Katie closer, adrenalin still humming through his body, and kissed her.

"Hey! What are you two doing?"

They jumped at the creaky voice shouting at them from the nearby porch. Scrambling to their feet, they looked over at the elderly man shaking his finger at them.

"You kids think you can just camp out on my wall and smooch?"

"Sorry," Griffin called.

"Smooch?" Katie asked. "Did he really say *smooch*?"

Grabbing each other's hand, they turned and fled, shaking with laughter. At the corner, they stopped to catch their breath.

"Still want to go to that movie?" asked Griffin.

"Sure, why not." She glanced at her watch. "We've got time to make the next showing."

"Because aren't your folks gone all day up in Denver?" He took a step closer, wrapping his arms around her waist. "We could hang out at your house. Watch a movie there."

"Are you trying to get me in trouble?"

"What trouble? We'll just be in the den. Eating popcorn and watching Star Wars for the bazillionth time."

Katie chewed her lip. "Well... I think it would be okay. I mean, they've never actually *told* me you couldn't come over when they're not home." She grinned up at him. "Promise to behave?"

"I'll be a perfect—" he began.

"Please," she begged, "don't say *angel*."

ഌ

"Did you hear that?" Katie lifted her head from where it rested on Griffin's chest, and peered over the back of the sofa toward the kitchen.

"Hear what?" Griffin propped himself up on one elbow from his prone position and smoothed his rumpled hair.

"Oh, no! That's my mom's car!"

"Oh, Fire!" He scrambled to his feet, almost dumping Katie on the floor.

"Go out the front," she hissed, tossing the empty soda cans into the bowl of leftover popcorn and sweeping stray kernels off the coffee table.

"Right." He snatched his shoes out from under the sofa and darted down the hall.

As he reached the entryway, he heard a key click in the door; he skidded to a halt. "By the Light!" he said in unconscious imitation of Basil. He spun around, his socks slipping on the tiled floor, and dashed back toward the den. "Katie, they're coming in the front," he whispered.

"Out the kitchen door! Go!" She shoved him ahead of her, still holding the bowl in one hand. Together, they shot across the hall.

Halfway across the kitchen, Griffin froze in mid-stride at the sound of a voice at the back door. Unable to stop in time, Katie slammed into him. The bowl flew from her hand, popcorn and soda cans spewing across the floor. Whirling around, he grabbed her arm, yanking her backwards. Just as they ducked into the hallway, Lewis Heflin stepped inside, Bear pushing past him. The dog pounced on the buttery kernels, gobbling them down with delight.

Pressed against the hallway wall, Griffin and Katie stared at each other in dismay. For a minute, the sound of Helen rummaging around the entryway closet vied with that of Lewis grumbling at the mess in the kitchen.

My bedroom, she mouthed in desperation, pointing toward the staircase. Griffin nodded and crept forward, Katie on his heels. Keeping low, they slipped up the stairs, then tiptoed along the upper hall and into her room.

"Just wait here. I'll figure something out," she whispered. Taking a deep breath, she smoothed her hair and forced a serene expression on her face; then she left, pulling the door closed behind her.

Griffin wiped his brow and glanced around. Wow. And Basil thinks *I'm* messy. Piles of clothes hid the bed and the swivel chair, while various books, her laptop, and empty plates covered the desk. Something pale and lacy peeked out from under a tee shirt on the bed. He stared for a moment, tilting his head for a better view. Reaching over, he eased the shirt aside, his fingers brushing against a pink brassiere.

He started to reach for it, then jumped, jerking his hand back at the rising sound of angry voices, Katie's shrill with frustration. As they grew louder, Griffin hesitated, then ran to the window. Tucking his shoes under one arm, he cranked it open and climbed out onto the steep roof, and then reached back in, closing it as much as he could.

Careful of the slippery shingles, he edged around the corner of the dormer and crouched down. As he listened, the bedroom door swung open. He heard Katie gasp as her mother stepped inside.

"And another thing, young lady. I want this room cleaned up. After you're done mopping the kitchen floor."

"Okay," Katie said in a weak voice.

I bet she thought I was still in there, thought Griffin. And that her mom was going to catch me in her bedroom. Glad I escaped when I did!

"Kathleen Heflin! Why is your window open? Are you trying to heat the entire state of Colorado?" Before Griffin could move, the window rolled closed with a snick.

He waited a few minutes, watching the sun balancing on the tops of the mountains. Well, he thought, I don't hear anything. I wonder if they went downstairs. Inching forward, he twisted around to peek inside. At that moment, his shoes tumbled from his grip. Rolling down the roof, one after the other, they disappeared over the edge of the gutter, landing on the front walk with a double thump.

Griffin smacked his hand on his forehead. Cursing under his breath, he started to tap on Katie's window, but hearing a familiar mechanical purr, he jerked his head around. He froze in horror.

He watched the Saab roll up the street and turn into their driveway. As he huddled in the lee of the dormer, he saw Basil step out. Oh, please, don't look over here, he prayed. He held his breath until his Mentor had disappeared into the house.

"That's it. I'm outta here." He stood up and walked down to the edge of the rain gutter. Leaning forward, he checked below, then stepped off the roof. Vanishing in mid-air, he reappeared as he landed in a crouch on the front lawn next to his shoes. He scooped them up and ran across the street to the safety of his porch. Panting, he looked back at the house he had just left. "Okay, that was *too* close!"

I better call Katie as soon as I can, he thought, as he balanced on one foot, tugging a shoe over each wet sock in turn. She'll be wondering how I got off the roof. I'll just tell her I jumped down. Make up some story about landing in a snowdrift or something. He nodded to himself, then opened the door and slipped inside. Easing it closed behind him, he turned around with a smile of relief.

And jumped, the air whooshing out of his lungs.

Basil stood waiting in the hallway, his arms crossed over his chest. "Why, hello, Tiro. Did you have a good flight?"

Chapter Twenty-Three

Griffin's Journal: Saturday, November 26th (cont.)

TALK ABOUT OVERREACTING! It wasn't like we were doing something we shouldn't have been doing.

I'm grounded for five days. I can't see Katie and he took my cell phone. And I had to go over and apologize to Mr. and Mrs. Heflin. *For pushing the boundaries of appropriate behavior in a deceitful manner* or something like that.

I never got a chance to tell him about rescuing that man. Think I'll wait on that.

I keep thinking about being in Katie's bedroom. Are they all pink?

Katie's Journal: Saturday, November 26th

Mom was mad, but Dad went ballistic! I can't see or talk to Griffin again until I'm, like, 30.

And I think we blew any chance of going to Carlee's party.

Katie's Journal: Thursday, December 1st

Finally!

We can see each other again! Dad said he can come over for dinner tonight. And it looks like we're both cleared to go to Carlee's party on Saturday.

Of course, Griffin was a total suck-up to my parents. But he is good at it, I'll give him that. He asked Dad a bunch of questions about that Kellsfarne manuscript during dinner. Got Dad to show him his copy.

Thought my dad was going to freak when Griffin read it. In Latin! He even said he thought there might be some errors in the Fitzwilliam translation, and that Basil could help.

What kind of teenager is fluent in medieval Latin?

Basil's Journal: Thursday, December 1st

Against my better judgment and under intense pressure from Lena (no doubt prompted by Griffin), I've decide to let him attend a party at the home of a friend of Katie's. Since the parents will be chaperoning it, she thought it would be a good experience for Fin.

And just how can partying with a bunch of human teenagers be a good experience for a young angel?

ꕤ

Griffin grinned as another leftover kernel popped and exploded out of the glass bowl on his lap and bounced off the back of Katie's head. She ignored him, continuing her conversation with Carlee. I really shouldn't be doing this, he thought, then tipped the bowl toward her and heated the bottom again with his cupped hands, his mouth twitching as more popcorn spewed out on her.

Katie glared at him over her shoulder. "Stop throwing popcorn," she hissed. "You're getting salt all over me." Picking a few stray ones off the sofa, she tossed them in the nearby fireplace. She whacked him on the arm as he laughed, then turned back to Carlee. "I can't take him anywhere," she said over the hum of voices in the crowded living room.

Her friend giggled and started to speak when a girl rushed up. "Hey, Carlee! Some juniors just came in. They're in the kitchen. Did you invite them?"

Carlee scrambled to her feet. "Oh, no! My parents'll kill me. They said only sophomores." She pushed her way through the throng, Katie on her heels, Griffin a few steps behind. They squeezed down the hall and into the kitchen.

Nash Baylor, flanked by several teammates, bent over the ice chest in the corner of the kitchen and snagged a soda can. He glanced at his friends. "You guys want one? Looks like they've got plenty." Grinning, he grabbed a few more and tossed them over, flicking the icy water off his fingers. He turned around as Carlee rushed into the kitchen. "Hey, Carlee. We heard about your party, so we thought we'd drop by," he said, leaning against the counter as he popped the top. His eyes widened when he spotted Katie behind her. "Oh, yeah," he murmured under his breath, giving his brown and white letter jacket a tug as he smiled at her. "Katie Heflin. If I had known you were here, I would have crashed it earlier."

"Sorry, Nash, b-but you guys weren't invited," said Carlee. "My mom and dad said just sophomores."

He looked over at her and snorted. "We're not doing anything—just having some sodas and talking with friends. So, chill."

She flushed and swallowed, taking another step forward. "I mean it. My parents are upstairs. So...so you need to leave,' she said in an unsteady voice.

"When we feel like it," Nash said. His buddies guffawed as he gestured around the kitchen. "This seems the place to be tonight. Plenty of snacks and good-looking girls. Pretty sweet, if you ask me."

"But you weren't asked," said a voice behind Katie. She turned her head as Griffin eased past her through the packed doorway and planted himself in front of Nash. For the briefest moment, she thought she saw a faint radiance surrounding Griffin. She blinked. And it was gone.

Griffin stared up at the taller boy, the room tomb-like as the crowd held its breath, waiting for the clash. "Look, Carlee said you weren't invited. And her parents said you weren't invited. Do you see a pattern here?" I'm really beginning to hate this guy, he thought.

Nash took a sip, slurping as he glared over the rim. "It's not your business, punk."

"And it's not your party, jerk," said Griffin. "Carlee asked you to leave. And you're scaring her. So leave."

"How are you going to make me?"

Griffin shrugged. "For you, I'd start with the basics. Like how to use a doorknob. They can be complicated for some people."

Nash flushed when his teammates snickered. He straightened, narrowing his eyes, and then flung the contents of his drink into Griffin's face.

The crowd gasped.

Griffin blinked, spitting soda and shaking his wet bangs out of his eyes. Now how did I know he was going to do that? he thought, swiping his face with his sleeve. Basil's going to be pissed, but what the heck. Without warning, he lunged and shoved Nash with both hands, a bit of Might judiciously applied.

The older boy staggered back on his heels, then crashed down, his elbow whacking a wooden chair and sending it skittering across the tile floor. He sat stunned, his face flushed with rage. "You're dead," he said softly. As he scrambled to his feet, one of his buddies grabbed his arm, jerking him to a stop.

"Dude! Some kid just went to get Carlee's dad. Come on!" The friend dragged Nash toward the back door; the other two were already waiting in the yard. Nash paused, a silent threat. Then, without another word, he disappeared into the night.

Griffin stared at the darkness through the open door for a minute, Might still tingling through his body, then walked over and slammed it shut with a thud. He blew out a deep breath and turned around, flexing his hands. "Whew!" he said with a crooked grin as Katie joined him. "Testosterone rush." His smile faded as he glanced back at the closed door.

Katie laid a hand on his arm, rubbing his tense muscles. "Were you really going to fight him?"

"What?" Griffin blinked and looked down at her. "Oh. Um ... I don't know. I was kind of hoping to avoid one." He frowned and shook his head. "But he shouldn't have upset Carlee like that."

"Thanks for standing up to him," said Carlee, squatting down and wiping the spilled soda with a paper towel. "And no offense, but Nash would've killed you."

"I don't think so," he said under his breath, then slung his arm around Katie's shoulders, squeezing as she started to tremble. "Hey! It's okay. It's all over and nothing happened."

"I was afraid you might get hurt."

"Oh, I'm pretty tough." *In some ways.* Griffin wrapped both arms around her and hugged her tight. "Do you want to go home?" he whispered in her ear.

Katie nodded. "Would you be hurt if we took off?" she asked, peeking at Carlee from Griffin's embrace. "We can stay and help you clean up if you want?"

Carlee sighed and shook her head. "Naw—go ahead. Molly's spending the night and we'll take care of it," she replied and glanced at Griffin. "Do you wanna dry off a little before going outside?" She gestured toward the hallway. "Just use the powder room." As he left, the girls made their way to the front door, lingering in the entryway.

"Are you parked far away?" Carlee asked.

"No, we're just at the end of the street. By that construction site." Katie looked around as Griffin appeared, his shirt dry, both their jackets under one arm. "Thanks again, Carlee. I'll see you Monday," she added as he helped her on with her jacket; she smiled up at him as he tugged her hair free of the collar.

Carlee watched wistfully. "Griffin, you don't have any brothers, do you?"

ꝏ

"Poor Carlee. She was so jazzed about this party," Katie said as they hurried up the block, their breaths billowing in the freezing air. "I can't believe Nash!"

"I can," said Griffin, then stopped and cocked his head for a moment. A dog barked once, then silenced. Tugging on her hand, he picked up the pace. "Let's move. I don't want you to get cold," he lied.

"What's wrong?" she asked in a low voice, biting her lip as she peeked over her shoulder at the quiet neighborhood.

"I thought I heard ... something." He scanned the street as he pulled her along. Reaching the edge of the dirt lot, they both sighed with relief at the sight of the Saab a few yards away.

Behind them, doors creaked as four figures stepped out of a nearby parked car and began heading toward them.

Griffin dropped Katie's hand and twisted around, facing the threat. Cursing under his breath, he fumbled for the remote in his pocket, then grabbed her hand and pressed the keys into it. "Run to the car. Get in and lock the doors." Grabbing her shoulders, he spun her around, ignoring her protests. "Go now!" He pushed her toward the vehicle, and then whirled back on guard, listening with one ear as her footsteps faded away. As the Saab's door slammed, he nodded to himself. "'First rule,'" he quoted, murmuring to himself, "'see to their safety. Second rule, see to their safety. Third rule, see rules one and two.'"

He watched as Nash and his friends sauntered over, forming a loose pack in front of him. For a moment, no one moved.

Then Griffin laughed. "You've gotta be kidding! This is the best you could come up with?" He shook his head. "I don't think this is such a good idea—someone's going to get hurt. I'm pretty sure, it won't be me."

"What the—" began Nash.

"Come on, Baylor. Just leave it, man," cautioned one of the other players. "We've got playoffs and a fight would get us suspended from it. Last thing we need right now."

"That only applies on school grounds," said Nash, lifting his chin. He took a step closer, crowding Griffin. "And even though this isn't school, it's time you learned a lesson. You won't be such a smart mouth after we're done with you." He snorted and added, "But don't worry about Katie. I'll make sure she gets home. Eventually."

Griffin's smile never reached his eyes. "I don't think she's that into you, dude," he said, bracing his feet. "And, by the way, your battle tactics suck. If you guys were really going to fight me, you would have ambushed me back there. By the car." He gestured with his head. "Two in front to stop my advance and two behind as rear guards. Then you could have effectively used your superior numbers to advantage." Basil would be so proud, he thought.

"I'm gonna—" began Nash.

"Now, with all this yakking," Griffin continued, "I'm on guard and the element of surprise is gone." He checked his watch. "Look. I really need to get Katie home. It's cold out here and she's got an eleven o'clock curfew, so we either go our separate ways or get this over with." Adding fuel to the flame, he couldn't resist one final jab. "I hope you guys play football better than you strategize."

Nash snapped. With a growl, he swung wildly. Griffin stumbled back, flinging up his hand. Nash howled as his fist collided against an invisible wall; he crumpled to the ground, rocking in pain as he cradled his broken wrist. Eyes watering, he looked up at his friends. "Kill him!" he rasped.

Griffin dove to one side, skidding to his knees, then cocked back an arm and punched his fist into the ground in front of him. The earth split with a groan, the crack racing toward the other players. He scrambled to his feet, watching as two of them teetered on the edge of the deep crevasse, then tumbled in. Three down, one to go, he thought, then spun around as the remaining attacker sprinted forward. Flicking a finger, he launched a fireball, skipping it off the player's head with a soft sizzle. As the boy cursed and slapped at his singed hair, Griffin sneezed. He wiped his nose with the back of his hand, then stepped back, eyeing Nash and his buddy as they dragged the trapped players up and over the lip of the trench. Yelling at each other in confusion over what had just happened, the four fled back toward their vehicle.

"That's it? Two minutes and it's all over?" called Griffin, unaware of Katie climbing out of the Saab behind him. "That's all you guys got?"

Reaching his car, Nash stopped, panting as he hunched against the back fender, his injured arm tucked inside his jacket. He looked past Griffin and glared at Katie.

"Your boyfriend's a freak," he screeched, spittle flying from his lips. He snarled in pain as his friends dragged him inside; the motor roared to life a second later. "A freak," he screamed once more before the door slammed shut.

The words hung in the air as they gunned away.

Griffin blinked. Oh, Fire! he thought in sudden dismay, watching with unseeing eyes as the car squealed around the corner. Katie! He swallowed and forced himself to turn and face her.

Katie stood beside the Saab's open door, the dome light casting half her face in shadow. Eyes wide, she gawked at Griffin, her mouth working silently as she shook her head from side to side. "What *are* you?" she finally whispered.

"Okay," he said, easing toward her and patting the air with his hands. "That was weird, I know. But I can explain ...." He stopped a few feet away when she lurched backwards.

"Get away from me," she cried, wrapping her arms around herself, shivering with fright and cold.

He tried again. "Can I at least say something? Please?" He took another step, then froze when she shook her head, her teeth chattering. "Let me drive you home, then. You're freezing. That's all I'll do. Drive you home. Or you can take the car yourself. Just leave it in our driveway. I'll walk."

"I'm not going anywhere with you! Not until you tell me what's going on. The truth, Griffin!"

"The truth about what?"

"About what I saw you do!"

"What do you think you saw?"

"You did ... something ... creepy," said Katie, starting to tremble again.

"Nah—it was just a fight, Katie. Guys get in fights all the time and—"

"Stop lying!" she screamed. "Tell me!"

What the heck do I do? he thought. I know Katie. She won't budge until I tell her. And I want to tell her. Let her know the real me. "You really want to know the truth?" he asked.

She nodded. "Yeah. Yeah, I do."

He looked up at the star-frosted sky, searching for courage, a bubble of dread pressing against his heart. Closing his eyes, he took a leap of faith. "Do you remember when I asked if you believed in angels?"

ꟷ

Humming contentedly, Basil checked the tea brewing in the old brown pot, then stopped and cocked his head at the rumble of the Saab pulling into the driveway. Goodness, he thought, they're home earlier than expected. He grimaced at the sound of car doors slamming shut followed by raised voices and footsteps racing away. Not good, he thought. A few moments later, the front door opened and closed. He pulled the filter out of the teapot and finished dumping the tea leaves in the garbage as Griffin stumbled into the kitchen.

Pouring his drink, Basil commented over his shoulder. "Party wasn't that fun, I take it?" When he didn't hear a response, he put the pot down and looked around.

Griffin hovered in the doorway, his jacket still on. "Basil?" His voice cracked; he licked his dry lips and tried again. "Basil, I have to tell you something, but don't get mad, okay?"

Why, in the name of all that is holy, do my Tiros always say that? Basil fumed silently. Especially when they know I'm going to explode! "Don't get mad about—"

"I told Katie."

"Told her what?"

"I told Katie," he repeated, staring at the floor. "I got in a fight and she saw ... she saw me."

Dismay clawed at Basil. "What did she see, Fin?" He stepped closer. "What do you mean—a fight?" he asked, eyeing Griffin for injuries.

"Katie saw me. What I did. During the fight. You know." He waved an arm in the air to illustrate, flames dancing briefly on the tips of his fingers. "She freaked out so I told her. And she said ..." He stopped and swallowed. "She said she never wants to see me again. That I've been lying to her all this time. About what I really was."

"By the Light, Griffin!" Basil threw his hands into the air. "I *knew* bloody well this was going to happen!"

Griffin winced. "You said you weren't going to get mad."

At that moment, the doorbell rang, followed by furious pounding. Basil shoved past him and headed down the hall, Griffin trailing behind. He flipped on the hallway light, and yanked the door open. Lewis Heflin stood there.

"What in blazes did your son do to my daughter, Raine?" he growled. "She came home—practically hysterical. Babbling some nonsense about your boy doing bizarre things with ... with ... fire! And the ground!" Lewis noticed Griffin standing behind Basil and glared. "I don't want him near Katie. Ever again!" He turned and stomped down the steps into the night.

Basil rubbed the bridge of his nose, then closed the door and leaned against it, his palm pressed against the wooden panel as he fought to keep calm. Taking a deep breath, he turned around and gazed at Griffin. "Let me guess—for some reason, one I do hope was well worth it, you used your abilities in front of Katie. She panicked. And then you admitted to being a Terrae Angelus. Am I correct?"

Griffin nodded.

"Did she truly believe you?"

"I don't know," he said hoarsely. "I mean, she thinks I'm not human." He looked away. "She thinks I'm a freak."

Basil sighed and moved toward Griffin; he caught the youth around the neck in a rough, one-armed embrace. He smiled when Griffin leaned against him. "I assume you're not too mature for a hug from your old Mentor, eh?" Basil reached up and cuffed him lightly on the head with his other hand.

"Sometimes, lad, it's hell being an angel."

Chapter Twenty-Four

Katie's Journal: Sunday, December 4th

Oh, God, I'm so confused! I don't know what to think. What to believe. Maybe he's mentally sick or obsessed or whatever. Is that why he kept talking with my dad about that manuscript? He told me he was one of those. Tera something.

Does Griffin really believe he's an angel?

Do I?

I don't know. I keep thinking about when he walked through the sprinkler. And saved Bear. How he popped all those balloons at the Festival.

The fight. And what he did.

Basil's Journal: Tuesday, December 6th

The first time is the most painful. Especially when it's someone we're close to. Especially when it's based solely on what we are. Most Terrae Angeli experience rejection, at least once in our long lives.

Lewis certainly reacted quite strongly, but I don't blame him. He was protecting his child and I understand that instinct. It's a shame, because he and Helen strike me as two humans who are open-minded enough to accept our existence, given Lewis' knowledge about the Kellsfarne.

Katie's Journal: Thursday, December 8th

I mentioned my theory to Dad today—that something is mentally wrong with Griffin. When he asked me why, I told him about Griffin claiming to be a tera angel or whatever it's called. It was weird. I mean Dad's reaction. He asked me to describe exactly what Griffin did. After I told him about the ground moving and the fire shooting up, he started asking me if I had ever seen anything else. So I told him about the other stuff. He did say that maybe he overreacted and that I could still see Griffin if I wanted to.

Don't know if I want to or not.

He and Mom are in the den with the door shut.

Basil's Journal: Sunday, December 11th

The lad's barely spoken a word all week and isn't eating or sleeping much. It's like the old Griffin all over again. I should chastise him severely for exposing our little secret, but he's already doing a fine job himself. Lena has visited several times, bless her, but he would hardly speak with her either.

However, Griffin has responsibilities. He is still a Terrae Angelus.

✽

Basil trudged up the stairs to Griffin's room. Knocking once on the half-opened door, he stepped inside and gazed at his Tiro spread-eagled on the unmade bed, fully clothed, staring out the window at the snow racing past. Time for a bit of tough love, thought Basil. Or he'll just sink deeper, if I know Griffin. And I do.

"Supper's ready, Fin."

Griffin kept his eyes fixed on the storm. "No, thanks."

"Refusing to eat is no longer an option." Basil waited for a moment, and then reached down and seized Griffin's arm, pulling him up and off the bed. "Up you get."

"Basil!" Griffin twisted free as soon as his feet touched the floor. "I don't feel like eating, okay?" He glared up at his Mentor.

Basil raised an eyebrow, then grabbed his arm and spun him around. Planting his hands on Griffin's shoulders, he propelled him out the door and down the stairs, the youth complaining all the while. Frog-marching him through the house, Basil steered him into the kitchen and parked him on a chair. Two bowls of vegetable soup steamed on the table.

"There," Basil said. "Now, that wasn't so difficult, was it?" He walked over to the refrigerator. "Care for juice?"

Griffin sat glowering at the soup, his eyes a brown fury. "I'm. Not. Hungry," he said through clenched teeth.

Basil yanked open the refrigerator door and grabbed the cranberry juice. He poured a glass and slammed it down, the liquid splashing onto the table. Griffin flinched. "And I said *eat*! We're on call, which means you'll be dressed, fed, and ready to serve and protect." He snatched his mug off the table for a coffee refill. Once at the counter, Basil sneaked a peek over his shoulder, then heaved a silent sigh of relief at the sight of Griffin eating reluctantly, one hand propping up his head. Finally! I thought I was going to have to tie him to the chair and pour soup down his stubborn throat. Putting the carafe back on the burner, he joined him at the table.

"So, tell me," he asked, sipping his coffee as he studied his apprentice. "Can you handle a mission if we're called? Because I would rather fly solo than take you along right now."

Griffin shifted uneasily at the thought of Basil alone on a mission. Without back up. "I'm good."

Basil leaned forward, resting his elbows on the table. "Look, Fin. I understand what you're going through. Truly, I do. But we have mortals depending on us, so I need you to angel up."

There was a long silence, and then Griffin blinked. "Did ... did you just say *angel up*?"

"I did," Basil replied blandly.

"That's awesome." Griffin chuckled, and then sighed and put down his spoon. He leaned back and looked at Basil ruefully. "I've been a real pain, haven't I?"

"To say the least. Though I won't deny I acted any better the first time it happened to me."

"You gonna tell me about her?"

"How old are you?"

"Sixteen."

"Nope."

"Fine. Be that way." Griffin picked up his spoon and took another mouthful of soup, then wrapped one hand around the bowl, warming his dinner. "So how long are we on standby?"

"All evening." Basil glanced out the kitchen window. "Things may get dicey with this storm."

Chapter Twenty-Five

"I CAN'T BELIEVE THEY'RE STILL HOLDING the Advent service," said Helen. She paused, stomping the snow off her boots before pushing through the doors of the small chapel. Stained glass windows, separated by arching beams, soared two stories above their heads. "How... pseudo-Gothic," she murmured to herself.

"Well, you know the College," Lewis said, pulling off his cap and tucking it into a pocket. "Nothing, and I do mean nothing, gets in the way of a tradition. If I weren't a new faculty member, I would have skipped tonight. But since I am, here we are." He led the way down the narrow aisle and selected a pew for his family. Shooing Katie in first, he joined his wife as they waited for the service to begin.

"I'm glad we could pry her out of her room," he whispered.

Helen nodded absently. She thought for a moment, and then turned to her husband. "Lewis. What if it's true?" she said, keeping her face averted from Katie. "You know. What we talked about the other day."

"I don't know. One part of me thinks it's absurd and Griffin is just delusional. While the other part of me would be delighted." He looked around, then chuckled. At Helen's unspoken question, he indicated a tall window set high between two massive pillars in the stone wall. Crafted from shades of blues and reds, browns and golds, a dark-haired angel rose above the earth, wielding a sword of fire.

"Does that remind you of anyone?" he asked. She smiled. Lewis glanced past her and caught Katie staring at the same window.

ꕥ

"Basil! We're up," Griffin yelled, snatching their jackets off the hallway hooks. "Fire at the College. Palmer Chapel. People trapped inside." He yanked open the front door as Basil thundered down the stairs. Side by side, they raced across the porch, vaulted over the railing, and vanished.

ꕥ

Screams ripped through the chapel as another burning beam crashed down, blocking the doors and setting their carved panels ablaze. Thick, heavy smoke swirled about as fire from the defective furnace fed on the century-old timbers. Lewis pushed his wife and daughter against the side wall, trying to protect them from the panicked crowd. Unable to find another exit, the congregation raced back and forth, shoving and trampling each other.

"Get on the floor," Lewis hollered. "More breathable air." Sheltered on one side by the stone wall, the Heflins lay flat; Katie was sobbing from fear.

Please, God, prayed Helen silently, please, God.

First one window blew out, then another, colored fragments spraying the room; people screamed as glass cascaded down. Snow and wind poured in, adding oxygen to the growing fire. Lewis scrambled to protect his wife and child with his body, wincing as a shard nicked his cheek.

A reverberating boom echoed over the pandemonium. The massive doors shuddered, then shuddered again, forced inward inch by inch; each blow from the outside causing them to ram against the blockage. For a long minute, all movement ceased; the only sounds were the roar of the flames and the wind screaming through the crack. Then, in a deafening crash, the doors exploded. Sparks shot upward as wood scraps and twisted hinges peppered the room; the burning beams flipped end over end and slammed harmlessly into the corners.

Two figures leaped through the opening and into the inferno.

Like a knight to battle, Basil charged down the aisle, parting the crowd with his long stride. Pointing upward with both hands, he aimed, Water gushing from his hands in powerful jets. As he made his way toward the front of the chapel, he thoroughly doused beam after beam, the droplets sizzling around him turning to steam and adding to the murky air. Reaching the altar, he spun around, wiping his fingers dry on his jeans as he looked back. "Griffin," he called. "Escort them out!"

Griffin nodded, already halfway down the aisle; his hair was tousled by flight and his face aglow with a fierce joy. A fireball blazed in one hand, the flames dancing on the tips of his fingers; he raised his arm and began shepherding the nearest group toward the exit. "No, ma'am," he said, ignoring questions and waving the congregation onward. "It's just a new type of flashlight. Nope, runs on solar. Now please head outside." He grinned and looked over, exchanging amused glances with

Basil. "Hey, I'm going to check out front," he yelled. "Make sure everyone's okay until the fire trucks get here."

The Mentor nodded, a look of pride on his face. And I was concerned he wouldn't rise to the occasion, he chided himself. I should have known. Shaking his head, he turned and glanced at the altar covering. "Oh, but too bad about the damage," he muttered, examining the delicately embroidered linen for several minutes.

"Basil! Hey, Basil!"

Alarmed, he looked around, then up. He frowned in confusion at the sight of his grinning Tiro perched on the highest windowsill among the shards of colored glass. The breeze ruffled his hair as he crouched on the stone ledge.

"Griffin! What in blazes are you doing up there?"

"Guess what I am?" Griffin asked, and then made a face, sticking out his tongue and crossing his eyes.

"A bloody idiot?"

"No! I'm a gargoyle!" Griffin huffed in exasperation and made a face again. "Get it?"

Basil groaned and rolled his eyes as Griffin gave a whoop, dove off the sill and vanished. Well, at least he's not sulking any more. "I thought you were out front," he said as Griffin appeared, landing with a thud on a nearby pew. "And off the furniture, lad."

He hopped down. "Oh, they're all right. Everyone's outside, standing around and talking about their close call."

"Um...." Basil stared over Griffin's shoulder, his gaze fixed on three figures staggering to their feet next to the far wall. "Not everyone."

As the first fire truck screamed to a stop outside, the Heflins made their way over to the waiting angels, Lewis in front, with Helen and Katie arm-in-arm behind him. As the five stood looking at one another, Griffin sneezed.

"God bless you," said Helen.

ജ്ജ

"How come *you* don't smell like smoke?" said Katie as she snuggled next to Griffin on one end of the sofa, sharing a blanket. "Thanks, Dad." She smiled up at her father as he handed her a cup of hot cocoa.

Lewis swiped at her sooty nose with a grin before asking, "Griffin? Cocoa or coffee?" He held a tray of hot drinks, working off nerves by helping Basil in the kitchen.

"No coffee!" called a voice from the kitchen. "He'll drive me insane all night!"

"Cocoa it is." Balancing the tray, he handed Griffin the other mug. "Careful, it's hot," he murmured, then laughed. "Guess I don't need to worry about that, do I?"

"Um...no, sir."

"Here, darling." Lewis handed another cup to Helen relaxing in a nearby chair, and then sank down on the other end of the sofa. "Basil put a little something in that."

"He read my mind," sighed Helen, adjusting the ice pack on her hand. "Thank goodness we walked away from that nightmare with only a cut on your face and a blistered palm for me." She smiled. "I mean, thank *you* and Basil," she said to Griffin.

"Just another day on the job, eh?" Basil sauntered in from the kitchen. He scrubbed half-heartily at his soot-stained shirt, and then flipped the hand towel over his shoulder as he sat down in the chair across from Helen. He smiled at the sight of Griffin and Katie wrapped in the blanket, their heads pressed together as they whispered to each other. An expectant stillness enveloped the room.

"So. Angels, huh?" Lewis began.

"Well, yes," said Basil.

"Terrae Angeli? Like in the Kellsfarne manuscript?" he checked.

"Just like," answered Griffin.

"Can you ... you know ... do something?" Katie asked, pushing her bangs out of her eyes.

Griffin's eyes crinkled. He reached over and cupped her mug with one hand, trying to keep a straight face as her cocoa began boiling. Letting go, he flicked a finger at the hearth. A blaze erupted, crackling as it danced across the logs. He stifled a sneeze.

"Now that's enough, Fin. You're just showing off." Basil winked at Katie.

"Basil, I have some questions ...." said Lewis, an eager expression on his face.

"All of them!" piped up Griffin. He looked around, grinning proudly until he noticed everyone's puzzled expressions. His smile faded. "What? You were going to ask how many angels can dance on the head of a pin, right?"

Basil winced. "What questions I can answer, I will," continued the Mentor, ignoring his Tiro. "However, Lewis, there are some theological questions that I cannot discuss with mortals."

"Of course. Say, would you mind if I ran home and got my copy of the Kellsfarne?"

"Mr. Lewis, we have a copy. Wanna use ours?"

At Lewis' nod, Griffin untangled himself from the blanket. He hopped up and stared at Katie. "Come help me look for it," he said, jerking his head toward the hallway. "I think it's upstairs." Pulling her to her feet, he led the way. The adults exchanged tolerant glances.

"I wonder how long it'll take them to find it?" mused Helen.

"Quite some time, I believe," Basil said, leaning back and stretching out his legs. "Since it's across the hall in my study."

ꟾ

Hurrying along the upper hallway, Griffin made a beeline to his room, Katie in tow. Once inside, they stood gazing at each other. Before he could speak, she burst into tears.

"Oh, Griffin!" she cried. "I'm sorry. I'm sorry I didn't believe you!" She sniffled, swiping at her face with her sleeve, leaving an ashy smear across her cheek.

"It's okay." He wrapped his arms around her, grateful to be holding her. "I just wish I could have told you right away," he murmured, then chuckled. "Because that would have *so* gotten me a date with you."

She laughed, tightening her arms around his neck as she snuggled against his shoulder. "Missed you," she said and sighed when he ran his fingers through her hair.

"Hold on tight," he whispered. Pulling her close, he took a deep breath, his face screwed up with concentration. As they rose in the air, he bent his head and kissed her, their feet hovering a few inches above the rug.

"Oh, wow!" Katie broke the kiss and peeked down. "How do you—

"Better not have that door closed, Tiro."

They both startled at the approaching sound of Basil's voice, hitting the floor with a thump. Griffin wiped his lips and Katie smoothed her hair in place just as the Mentor stuck his head through the doorway, a sheet of paper in one hand. He waved it at them.

"Looking for this?" Katie blushed crimson as Griffin closed his eyes in embarrassment. "So if you're quite finished getting re-acquainted, Lewis is chomping at the bit downstairs." Basil nodded toward the stairs. "Come on, you two."

When they reached the main hall, he paused. "Katie, go on ahead, please. We won't be but a minute." As she joined her parents, he entered the study, Griffin on his heels.

Basil motioned for him to step closer. "I want you to be circumspect with Mr. Heflin," he whispered. "He's quite excited about this interview with an angel and may ask some questions we're not allowed to answer."

"Circumspect?" asked Griffin in a low voice.

"Cautious, wary, guarded ...." said Basil.

"Okay, I got it." Griffin quickly interrupted him before he picked up speed. "Well, I do!" he said, defending himself against Basil's stern expression.

"Cheeky."

ꙮ

"So you help people. Rescue them—like tonight?" asked Lewis, perched on the edge of his seat, a yellow writing tablet balanced on his knee. He leaned forward and studied the manuscript on the coffee table. Griffin and Katie snuggled together at the other end of the sofa while Helen relaxed nearby.

"When we can, yes," said Basil, walking around to refill Helen's cup. "Not every mission is successful, however." He sat back down across from her.

"Have you had missions where you couldn't save someone?" asked Helen.

The Terrae Angeli nodded, exchanging glances.

"So what do the other angels do?" The professor paused to check the Kellsfarne. "The celestial angels, I mean."

Basil shook his head. "I am sorry, but I'm not at liberty to discuss them."

Lewis made a quick note, scanned the manuscript, and then continued. "So it says here there are four ranks." He peered over his reading glasses at them. "Which one are you?"

"I am a Mentor. Which means beside my role as a guardian angel, I also train Tiros. That's what Griffin is. It's similar to an apprentice."

"Like a knight and his squire," said Katie.

Basil lifted an eyebrow. "Excellent analogy, Miss Heflin." He inclined his head. "And just as a knight was a warrior for the king, he was also responsible for the education of his squire. To prepare *him* for knighthood."

"What happens then?" asked Helen. "When Griffin finishes his apprenticeship. Do you two split up?"

"Not necessarily. Mentors and Tiros often pair together. As brothers-in-arms, you might say. Fin and I have talked about it." He smiled at Griffin, who grinned back. "With our different Elements, we complement each other. It makes for an effective team in the field."

Lewis scribbled furiously. "Okay—the four elements. Tell me about those."

Basil started to speak, but then turned to Griffin. "Why don't you explain?"

"Well, each Terrae Angelus is created from one or more of the ancient elements," Griffin said. "Earth, Fire, Wind, and Water." He indicated his Mentor. "Basil's a Wind and Water. That means he channels those elements, but also those elements have an influence on him. Even in his physical appearance. If you ever saw a bunch of us together, you could tell who's what."

"Your food allergies," said Helen. "Are those due to your ... element? Elements?"

"Yes, ma'am. That's why I can't eat animals from land and Basil can't eat seafood or fish. From the water."

Katie studied Griffin. "You're Earth and Fire, right?" He nodded. "So all that stuff with the fire and the ground during the fight with Nash was you? Controlling those elements? Can you handle both at the same time?"

"Barely. Basil's really good at it. I've tried a few times, but it always wipes me out."

"Beside controlling those elements," Helen continued, "do you have other abilities?" Lewis flipped to a new page.

Griffin glanced at his Mentor, eyebrows raised. Basil crooked a finger. "Let me chat with my Tiro. Excuse us, please." He rose, grabbing the coffee carafe as he headed toward the kitchen; Griffin trailed behind after collecting empty mugs.

"What do you want me to tell them? About Might? And flying? You *know* they're going to ask about flying," said Griffin. He rinsed the cups and placed them in the dishwasher.

Basil set the carafe back on the burner and leaned against the far counter, pondering. Griffin hoisted himself up on the other, kicking his heels as he stifled a yawn.

"Tired, lad?"

"A little. What a day, eh?" They both chuckled at his unexpected imitation of Basil.

"So what to tell them." Basil clicked his tongue as he debated, then came to a decision. "We'll keep Might use and flying under wraps for now."

Griffin grimaced, scratching the back of his head. "Um ... Basil? That might be a little hard."

"Why? Did you ... Griffin!" He growled in frustration. "When?"

"Earlier this evening. When we were upstairs in my bedroom." He spread his arms. "But it was only for a second!"

"That's what they all say."

Basil's Journal: Monday, December 12th

Miraculous event.

Griffin and I rescued the Heflins yesterday evening during a fire at the College. Which, of course, led to a late night question-and-answer session. All is well between the sweethearts.

I know Lewis will have more questions. He ceased only because Griffin and Katie fell asleep.

Lewis was fascinated by the differences between Terrae Angeli and celestial angels, as well as Terrae Angeli and humans. Helen was more curious about the similarities. She's quite fond of Griffin and asked questions about his apprenticeship, how I train him, his upcoming Proelium. She's as concerned about it as we are.

I'm not certain what will happen in the future—having neighbors who know our true identity might be a problem.

It might also be a blessing.

Chapter Twenty-Six

"So did anyone get hurt?" asked Carlee, slamming her locker closed.

"No, not really." Katie winced as the final bell clanged over her head. "An older guy needed oxygen, but that was about it. The chapel's pretty messed up. Dad said some of those stained glass windows were over a hundred years old and they can't ...." She stopped when Carlee looked at the hall clock and groaned.

"Oh, man! I gotta go finish my science lab." She grabbed her pack and scurried away. "See you tomorrow," she yelled over her shoulder as she shot through the crowd and around the corner.

Katie made her way through the halls and out into the courtyard; the wings of the bronze mascot in the center of the square were gilded by the afternoon sun. Her stride faltered when she noticed a dark-haired figure sitting cross-legged on top of the low wall. "Griffin! What are you doing here?"

He beamed at her. "Hey! I guessed right!" He hopped down from the wall as Katie walked over.

"Guessed right about what?" she asked, taking his hand.

"Which door you'd come out. I remember you mentioning once that you went home this way, so I took a chance." Grabbing her backpack, he slung it over his shoulder, then linked their fingers together. "Come on, I'm kidnapping you." He tugged her along, heading out of the courtyard toward the busy street corner, the high school traffic whizzing around them.

"Oooh, I love being kidnapped! Where are we going?" Katie smiled a greeting as several girl friends drove past. She rolled her eyes when they wolf-whistled at Griffin through open windows.

"Oh-Be-Joyful," he said, waving back at the girls, to their delight. "I've developed a serious espresso addiction and Basil's starting to cut me off after two cups." He paused, holding Katie away from the curb as two more cars full of teens blasted through the intersection a second after the light turned red.

"I better text Mom," she said over the roar of traffic. "Just to let her know." Katie dropped Griffin's hand and dug into her pocket.

"Hey, do that on the other side. The light's about to change." Griffin jogged across, then halted halfway and waited on the median. He glanced back. "Too late," he yelled. "Just wait for the next one!"

"Control freak," she muttered, her thumbs flying. She pressed send, then stowed the phone away as she dashed across the street. "You know what?" she called as she ran toward him, "I think I can handle crossing the—"

Tires shrieked, the front end of the sedan dipping down from the force of the driver slamming both feet on the brakes. Katie froze, her mouth wide with terror. The car skidded toward her, the grill a shark's mouth as it filled her vision.

She gasped, the air whooshing out of her lungs as Griffin plowed into her, lifting her off her feet. He spun around, clasping her in his arms and shielding her body with his. They flew through the air, over the car's hood, past the gutter, and landed on the sidewalk with a bone-jarring thud.

Her teeth snapped together as they bounced, then slid across the concrete. When they finally stopped, she found herself sprawled on top of Griffin, staring down at him. He grinned up at her and shook his head in exasperation.

"So what part of '*wait for the next light*' didn't you get?"

Chapter Twenty-Seven

Basil's Journal: Monday, December 19th

I DON'T BLOODY BELIEVE IT!

Nicopolis is overseeing Griffin's Proelium!

I wonder how many strings he pulled to achieve *that*!? I went to Command and insisted on another Mentor. I tried every argument, even demanded to speak with Mayla. But even she seemed to think I'm overreacting and that the bad blood between Nicopolis and us is nothing to worry about. Old news, as she said.

Doesn't she remember how vindictive he can be?!

Even though I'm not allowed to observe, I'll make sure I'm right outside afterwards to confirm the outcome.

I'll never forget the look on Griffin's face when I told him. Will he *ever* be free of his demons?

ஐ

The swing creaked as Griffin perched on the rim of the tire, his legs dangling inside. I wonder why mid-day is the loneliest time in a park? he thought. Grabbing the chains on either side, he leaned back, rocking as he gazed at the world upside down, his hair brushing the dirt. He frowned in exasperation as he spotted a tall figure sauntering across the playground toward him.

Coming closer, Basil raised an eyebrow and peered down at Griffin's upturned face. "Getting a different perspective?"

"Nah, just ... thinking." Griffin pulled himself upright. "Did you need me or is this just a Mentor thing?"

"It's completely a Mentor thing. Mind if I join you?" Basil leaned a shoulder against the support poles, his hands jammed into his jean pockets, enjoying the winter sun. "I never would have pegged you for a swing type," he said. "Always thought you were more of a slider." He nodded toward to the metal slide nearby.

"This is where I first kissed Katie," Griffin admitted, a faint blush on his cheeks.

Basil studied the contraption more closely. "Not a bad strategy. But then strategy has always been one of your strengths. Something to remember tomorrow, eh? So don't let Nicopolis shake you."

"I can't help it. If I fail..." he trailed off, staring across the park. "I won't do it, you know."

"You won't do what?"

"I won't become mortal." Griffin's knuckles whitened as he tightened a hand around the chain. Swinging his legs around, he hopped off the tire and walked away, stopping after a few feet. He peeked out of the corner of his eye as Basil ambled over. Side by side, they stood gazing at High Springs' famous peak.

"If it'll make you feel better, Fin, then I'll resign, too. And we'll be mortals together."

Griffin shook his head. "Thanks, but no way! They're not going to screw both of us." He sniffed, and then tugged his shirt out from under his down vest and wiped his nose on its tail.

"Griffin, would you stop doing that? It's disgusting!"

"Want me to use my sleeve?"

"Have you ever thought of a handkerchief?"

"This is the twenty first century. In America. *Nobody* owns a handkerchief."

They both laughed, and then Basil clapped a hand on Griffin's shoulder. "Let's walk over to your coffee shop. The one with the heavenly name? We need to talk about tomorrow."

They left the park and strolled through the neighborhood, Griffin taking two strides for every one of Basil's. As they reached downtown, the Mentor cleared his throat.

"Focus on your strategy. Offense more than defense," said Basil. "Try to determine which Element Nicopolis is using as quickly as you can." Griffin nodded. "And keep *him* guessing. Don't just use one Element—use everything you've got," Basil advised. "Change them around. But one at a time, of course."

"Right," said Griffin, rubbing a temple with one hand. I wish he'd quit lecturing, he thought. This is really not helping!

Basil plugged away. "Now as far as Might use is concerned, try—" he began, then stopped as Griffin slammed to a halt in the middle of the busy sidewalk.

"Stop. Just ... stop it." Griffin clenched his fists by his sides. "Basil, don't you think I've gone over all this stuff myself these last few months? I'm not clueless, you know. I have learned *something* over the last three years as your apprentice!"

Basil took Griffin's arm, pulling him aside and closer to the wall of a building. He waited as two businessmen walked past, then spoke in an undertone. "I certainly didn't mean to suggest otherwise. And if I appeared to cast doubts on your abilities, it was not my intent. My apologies for any offense given."

Groaning with frustration, Griffin slumped against the building and ran both hands through his hair. "I hate it when you take the high road," he muttered. "It makes me feel like a spoiled brat."

He pushed off the wall and continued up the block, Basil beside him. Reaching Oh-Be-Joyful, he held the door open for his Mentor. "Sorry. I know you're just trying to help," he said, then grinned when Basil cuffed him good-naturedly as they entered. He hurried over to place their order while Basil paused at the newspaper rack. As Griffin reached the front, he froze at the sight of a brown and white letter jacket and groaned silently. Just what I *so* don't need right now.

A few feet away, Nash Baylor turned from the counter, his drink halfway to his mouth. Spotting Griffin, he curled his lip. "Hey, it's the neighborhood freak."

"Hey, it's the neighborhood invalid," Griffin replied. He eyed the cast peeking out from the older boy's sleeve. "I heard you missed the playoff game. Broken wrist, right?"

Nash narrowed his eyes. He slammed his coffee down and stalked over to Griffin, crowding him. "Still a smart mouth, huh?"

Griffin snorted. "At least you got one out of two right."

Both combatants glared at each other, neither giving ground as the girl behind the cash register wrung her hands anxiously.

"Is there a problem here?" Basil appeared behind Nash, a newspaper tucked under one arm.

"None of your business," Nash responded over his shoulder, keeping his eyes fixed on the younger boy; he frowned when Griffin choked back a laugh. "What's so funny?" he demanded, then yelped when a stream of water spilled down the back of his shirt. Shoulders hunched from the chilly touch, he whirled around and looked up. Basil waited, his face serene.

"Was that you?" Nash snarled.

"Was that me what?"

"Did you just dump water on me?"

"No, I did not dump just water on you," Basil said. I'm quite certain there were bits of ice, too, he thought. "Perhaps you were imagining things." He cocked an eyebrow. "It's not the first time, eh?" he said with a smile as he casually took a step forward.

Nash's mouth twisted. He started to speak, then pushed past Basil and stormed out of the shop. The Mentor watched for a moment, and then turned back toward Griffin. Raising a finger, he leaned forward. "Don't you *ever* do what I just did," he said under his breath. "That's not what our abilities are for. Understand?"

Griffin nodded, his eyes dancing. "Sure, Basil. Whatever you say." Trying to keep from smiling, he murmured under his breath. "And the high road is now under construction."

Chapter Twenty-Eight

KATIE SIGHED AND ROLLED OVER, knocking a stack of folded jeans off the foot of her bed as she burrowed deeper under her comforter. Her eyes flew open as she heard a light tapping at her window. Lifting her head, she stared, trying to penetrate the darkness; the thumping of her heart almost drowned out the voice hissing her name.

"Katie. It's me."

With a gasp of relief, she flung back the cover, stumbled across the room, and pulled up the blinds. Griffin stood balanced outside on the roof, almost invisible in dark tee shirt and sweatpants. He stepped back as she cranked the window open.

"What are you ... Wait, how did you get up here?" she whispered.

Griffin grinned. "How'd you think?" He nodded over his shoulder.

She peered across the street at the sight of his open window, the drapes fluttering in the night breeze. "That is so *cool*," she breathed, then motioned for him to come in.

He crawled through the window, hopping down on bare feet, and then reached back and cranked it closed. Turning around, he whistled softly. The streetlight illuminated the room enough for him to notice Katie's baggy tee shirt and boxer shorts. Short boxer shorts. He stared at her legs. "I have *got* to come visit more often at night."

"Yeah. Right. If Dad finds you here, angel or not, he'll kill you."

"He'll have to catch me first." He flapped his arms up and down, rising up on his toes.

They burst out laughing. Shushing each other, they flopped down on Katie's bed, smothering their faces in the pillows. Breathless, they rolled on their sides and smiled at each other.

Griffin reached over and stroked her hair off her cheek, tucking it behind her ear. He leaned on an elbow and kissed her on the tip of her nose, then sat up on the edge of the mattress.

She joined him, tucking one leg under her and snuggling against his shoulder. Taking his hand in both of hers, she compared them. "You're always so warm and tan. Even in the winter," she marveled. "Is that because you're a ... um ... you know."

"Earth and Fire? Yup." Linking their fingers, he glanced sideways. "You sure it doesn't bother you? What I am?" he asked again.

"You'll always be *Griffin* to me. That won't change. No matter how many times you ask."

He opened her hand wide and kissed her palm. Looking over at her desk, he noticed a stack of textbooks. "I better not keep you up. Which final exams do you have tomorrow?"

"Math and English. Those are my last ones."

They sat silently in the dark for a few minutes, leaning against one another. "And what time is your ... test?" she asked.

"Mid-afternoon. But I probably won't get home until late." He let go of her hand and hunched forward, resting his elbows on his knees, his head bowed.

"You'll pass. I know it."

"I hope so," he said. "Because I can't—" He stopped and stood up. Running a hand through his hair, he walked over to the window and stared at the lights of the city.

"Hey, Griffin?" she asked tentatively. "Are you allowed to tell me about it? I mean, what's it like?"

Griffin turned. "The Proelium?" Walking over to her desk, he grabbed the chair and spun it around, straddling it with his arms draped over the back. "Well, it's really pretty simple. There's this huge circle, usually drawn in the dirt. The Tiro starts in the center, the Mentor at the edge. The goal is for the Tiro to get out of the circle. He or she can use any method, any ability, and any strategy to escape, except flight. The Mentor, to keep it fair, can only use one Element. Nothing else. They're not allowed to change Elements halfway through or anything like that." He shrugged. "And that's about it."

"Do you have a time limit?"

"Two hours. Or until the Tiro gives up." *Or passes out. Or fails.*

"Can you get hurt?"

"Yeah, it gets rough. But that's part of our training, so it's not as bad as it sounds. Think about what your soldiers go through during boot camp. It's like that," he explained. "I mean we don't maim or kill each other. There wouldn't be any Terrae Angeli left if we did that."

"So, is it really true? About what happens if you ... you know? Don't make it?"

Griffin nodded.

She hesitated. "Would it be so bad? Being a human?"

"I don't know." He ran a thumb along the scar on his lip as he thought. "Sometimes, when I'm with you, I wish I was just a guy. And we could do stuff. Go to school together. Have *normal* dates." They both smiled. "You know—regular human things. Maybe even think about a future together."

"I think about those things, too," Katie said softly.

"But then I go on a rescue mission with Basil." He looked over and gazed out the window at the stars. "And I see the good we can do. For people. Katie, it's the biggest rush in the world," he said, his voice deepening with passion. "Being a guardian is the whole reason I'm here on Earth. And if I'm not a Terrae Angelus, then I'm not anything." He sighed and stood up, pushing the chair under the desk. "I better get back. I just wanted to see you for a minute." Griffin stepped over to the window, cranked it open and squeezed through.

Katie jumped up. As she reached the sill, she stretched out a hand and cupped his chin, planting a kiss on his cheek. "Good luck," she whispered.

He smiled. Then, bending his knees, he surfed down the steep roof, his bare feet leaving furrows in the snow as he picked up speed. Reaching the edge, he vanished. A moment later, he reappeared, landing on his roof. With a final wave, he pushed aside his drapes and slipped inside.

ꕥ

Griffin made his way across the backyard, the morning frost crunching underfoot and the reluctant dawn highlighting the tips of the mountains. A tall figure lounged on the bench, steam rising from a coffee mug in his hand. Griffin stepped over Basil's long legs and sat down next to him. "When did you get up?" he asked his Mentor.

"Some time ago." Basil straightened up and held out his mug to Griffin, who wrapped a hand around it, warming it. "Thanks," he murmured. "I've been sitting here trying to think of some profound, insightful words to say to you today. Something powerful. You know. The kind they put on motivational posters."

"And?"

"Nothing. Not a thing." Basil shrugged and leaned back, burrowing deeper into his heavy jacket. He chuckled. "Do you remember the time you almost burned up that tree?" he asked, pointing at the spruce in the corner.

Griffin smiled. "I was so scared you were going to get mad at me. Instead you just put it out. Then moved on with the lesson." He sat for a while, thinking about those early days as he watched Basil swirl his coffee around his mug. His smile faded; he cleared his throat, trying to get past the sudden lump in it.

"Um ... Basil?" He finally got the words out and waited until the Mentor looked up. "I... uh... just wanted to say that whatever happens, I..." he stopped, unable to continue.

"I know, Fin. I know."

ꟈ

The bell rang as Katie slid into her seat. She caught a glimpse of Nash several rows away, avoiding her, his cast resting awkwardly on his desk. *I'm still surprised he and his friends haven't said anything,* she thought. *Probably because they either don't believe what happened or they don't want to admit getting beat up by one guy.*

As the teacher passed out the exam, Katie dug through her backpack, locating a number two pencil and her calculator. She stared at the first problem as she tapped her pencil against her teeth, trying to concentrate, trying not to think about Griffin. Under her desk, she crossed her fingers.

Chapter Twenty-Nine

GRIFFIN SLAMMED FACE FIRST INTO THE GROUND, the dust billowing up from the dirt floor. Wheezing from the impact, he rolled over, blinking away the blood from a cut slicing through his eyebrow. His vision swam in and out of focus as he stared up at the warehouse's high windows, their tiny panes coated with grime and the afternoon snowfall.

"Now there's a familiar sight," said a cold voice. Out of the corner of his eye, he watched as Nicopolis ambled around the outside of the circle, his gray suit and pale face making him almost invisible in the dim light. "You cowering on the ground. If memory serves, I believe tears come next."

Without a word, Griffin lurched to his feet. Ignore him, he said to himself. Just concentrate on getting out of here. He took a deep breath, then another, his injured ribs creaking in protest. Shifting his weight off his wrenched knee, he winced as he straightened it, trying to decide which tactic to use next.

"Well? Do *something*. I'm finding this rather tedious." Nicopolis glanced at his watch. "Unless you wish to yield. It's been well over an hour and I, for one, would like to go home."

"No. I'm not giving up," Griffin said through dry lips. He feinted toward one side, and then stumbled back, barely dodging another blast of Wind.

Nicopolis lowered his hand and tilted his head. "Personally, I think you'd make a fine human. With your lack of abilities, you're practically one already."

"That would be a dream come true for you, wouldn't it?" Griffin panted as he eyed the nearby line scratched in the dirt. "If I fail?"

"Why, yes! In fact...." Lifting both hands, Nicopolis smiled.

A gale ripped through the building. Griffin staggered backwards, blinded by dirt and debris. Struggling to breathe, he caught his balance and bent over, leaning into the wind, one arm raised to protect his face. He squinted, scanning the warehouse. As he watched, Nicopolis disappeared momentarily behind a cloud of dust.

Move, you idiot! he yelled at himself. While he can't see you! With a gasp, Griffin hobbled toward the circle. Halfway, he cried out as a windblown plank whirled through the air and slammed into his injured knee.

"Son of a ...," he breathed, tears of pain seeping down his face. He crumbled to the ground, cradling his limb. Gritting his teeth, his leg throbbing in rhythm with his pounding heart, he stared at the edge of the ring a foot away.

A mile away.

I got to find some way to slow him down, he thought, so I can reach that circle. For a moment, Basil's voice echoed in his ears, urging him to think, think! A vision of the quagmire in their back yard flashed through his mind. Maybe, just maybe ....

Rising up on his elbows, Griffin inched forward, and then made a show of collapsing in exhaustion. Come on, he thought, take the bait. Squeezing his eyes tight, he felt the wind die down. Stillness filled the enormous space, and then shoes shuffled across the floor and halted by his head.

"I do so regret Basil's not here," Nicopolis said. "I believe I owe him an *I-told-you-so.*" His voice grew louder as he leaned over to gloat.

At that moment, Griffin sucked in a deep breath and rolled over on his back, flinging out a hand. Flames exploded with a roar from his fingertips. Nicopolis threw his arm up, shielding his face as he stumbled back. Recovering, he sent a deluge of water, attempting to extinguish the blaze. The two Elements clashed in perfect balance.

Fire versus Water.

What the heck is he doing? Griffin thought as his concentration wavered. He's not allowed to switch Elements! He swore under his breath, almost losing control, and then lurched up to one knee, his arm shaking from the force of Nicopolis' torrent. Water began pooling between them. Griffin watched the puddle spread, steam billowing around them. "Not yet, not yet," he muttered, his arm trembling harder. "Just a little deeper."

"You're only postponing the inevitable!" Nicopolis shouted over the din.

Griffin ignored him. He glanced once more at the muddy pool, judging its size. Lifting his other hand, he brought his fist down like a hammer.

Shock waves rippled the surface of the pool like a tsunami. As they reached the other side, the ground under Nicopolis bucked, flipping him forward into the large puddle. With a yelp of surprise, he landed on his hands and knees. Before he could move, Griffin reached down and dug into the earth, curling and uncurling his fingers; the pool vibrated violently, mixing the earth and water into a thick muck.

Nicopolis thrashed about, unable to rise. With a grunt, Griffin lurched to his feet and spread both arms wide. Flames poured from his hands. Twin streams of fire raced each other around the puddle, enclosing the water and blowtorching the clay. It hardened around Nicopolis, trapping his hands and feet.

"Sorry about your suit," called Griffin over the inferno, then dropped his arms. He limped toward the edge, black spots flickering across his vision; with a gasp of triumph, he dragged his lame leg across the line, breaking the circle. As his Fire died down, he paused and looked back. Nicopolis twisted frenetically, attempting to break the clay's hold. Spittle flew from his mouth as he bellowed at Griffin.

The young Terrae Angelus grinned. He staggered back to scuff the line once more in victory, then hobbled away. Reaching the metal door, he grabbed the heavy handle and yanked it back, grimacing with the pain from his damaged ribs. He tugged it open and slipped through into the storm.

Sucking in a lungful of chilled air, he slowed down and wiped his brow, leaving a smear of dirt and blood. He looked around the parking lot, tremors beginning to rack him. I swear, if Basil doesn't show up soon, I'm going to fall down right here in the snow and go to sleep. Limping further from the building, Griffin blinked, struggling to keep his eyes open; his teeth started to chatter. "Oh, this is going to be a bad one," he said, wrapping his arms around his torso, shivering.

Behind him, the door was thrown open, ripped off its hinges and flung aside, landing several feet away with a deafening boom. Nicopolis stormed out, covered in filth. Fired clay, like bits of pottery, clung to his shredded sleeves and pant legs.

"Oh, crap!" Griffin rocked back, then tripped over the torn asphalt and fell. Rolling over with a groan, he gazed upward, snowflakes dusting his face with cold kisses. His head flopped to one side. As the world darkened around him, he squinted at an odd cloud billowing in from the south, flying against the wind and low to the ground. Lightning illuminated the interior in familiar shades of white and blue.

"About time you showed up," Griffin murmured, and then closed his eyes.

Chapter Thirty

Katie's Journal: Wednesday, December 21st

SNOWING HARDER NOW. Griffin's still not back. Mom and I went over before dinner, but they weren't home.

God, let him be okay.

༺༻

Flipping a hand towel over his shoulder, Basil picked up the bowl of warm water, balanced the first-aid kit on top, and hurried back upstairs to Griffin's bedroom. He placed the bowl and supplies on the bedside table, and then clicked on the lamp, pushing shadows into the corners. Taking a seat on the edge of the bed, he gazed down at the motionless figure sprawled on top of the covers. Ah, lad, he thought. I had no doubt.

After a moment, he dipped the cloth into the water, wincing as he dabbed at the cut angling through Griffin's right eyebrow. "Head wounds tend to bleed like the devil," he said aloud. "You might require a few stitches." After cleaning the injury, he examined it more closely. "Or perhaps not. A butterfly bandage or two should do the trick. You'll have an impressive shiner tomorrow, though," he added as he rummaged through the kit. After applying the dressings with a gentle touch, he cleaned the dried blood off Griffin's face and neck.

"You understand, of course, that this would all be a great deal easier if you were conscious," Basil complained good-naturedly, "or even semi-conscious." He watched for a moment, frowning at the hitch in Griffin's breathing. Lifting up the grimy shirt, he shook his head. "Bloody marvelous," he muttered. "Cracked ribs, too." He clasped the youth's shoulders and eased him upright; Griffin flopped like a rag doll as Basil leaned him forward to pull the hoodie over his head and off his limp arms. He tossed it aside, then kept Griffin in place with one hand while he wrapped wide elastic bandages tightly around his torso. Fastening the ends, he lowered him back down, then pressed his palm over the bandages, closing his eyes as he sent healing Might help along the injured bones. "That should speed things up. You'll still be sore for a few days, however."

After removing Griffin's shoes, he unfolded a spare comforter and tucked it around the young angel, mindful of his injured knee. Worry etched Basil's face as he stared at Griffin's cold, pale skin and slack mouth. He sighed. "I'm finding this one-sided conversation a bit of a bore. So anytime you wish to wake up would be fine with me. I'm eager for the details," he said, then chuckled. "I had to *encourage* Nicopolis to inform me of the outcome." He smiled briefly at the memory. "He could scarcely bring himself to admit you actually passed your Proelium." Wiping his hands on a clean corner of the towel, Basil glanced out the window as a gust rattled the glass; snow hissed past. Well, I best ring Lena, he thought, then brew some more coffee. It's going to be a long night.

ꟃ

The doorbell chimed just as Lena reached the foot of the stairs. She walked over and set the tray down on the bench, wiped her hands on her apron, and opened it.

"Is he okay? Did he pass?" asked Katie anxiously as Lena ushered her into the hallway.

"Good morning, Katie. Yes, he was successful." The older woman paused, then added, "But no, Griffin's not well." Lena raised a hand. "And before you start peppering me with questions, why don't we take breakfast to Basil, yes? He's been awake all night." She picked up the laden tray and waited as Katie hung her jacket on the coat hook. They climbed the stairs, and then hurried along the corridor, their footsteps echoing through the quiet house.

"When did you get here, Miss Weiss?"

"Oh, early this morning."

Reaching the bedroom, Lena entered and carried the tray to the desk. Katie hesitated in the doorway, then taking a deep breath, she slipped inside.

Basil relaxed in a chair on the far side of the bed, reading a book by the brilliant morning light, his blue eyes and white hair a reflection of sky and snow. Katie barely noticed him. She stared down at Griffin buried under the cover, his eyelashes black crescents against his colorless skin. Her gaze traveled from the dressing on his forehead past the swollen eye to the mottled bruises on his cheek and jaw. She stood there blinking back tears until Basil cleared his throat.

"He's a bit of a mess, eh?" he said. She glanced over at the Mentor. He smiled wearily at her, then brightened when Lena handed him a steaming mug.

"Oh, thank you," sighed Basil, reaching for the coffee and hot bagel she offered. After a few sips, he placed the mug on the windowsill next to him and tore into the chewy bread. Wiping jam off his knuckle, he nodded at the girl hovering nearby. "You can sit with him."

She moved closer and balanced on the edge of the mattress, laying a hand on Griffin's covered arm. "What happened?"

"I wish I knew the details. By the time I arrived, Fin was like this, outside in the storm. Nicopolis told me very little before he...fled." He smiled to himself.

"Did he do this to Griffin?"

"Partially. But the lad also over-extended himself by using both Elements at once."

"What do you mean?"

"It's like flooding a car's engine. When you give the engine too much gas, it stalls and then quits. Griffin used both Earth and Fire at the same time, which overloaded his system, you might say. That's why he's so cold."

"When will he wake up?"

"He'll wake up ... when he wakes up. But you should talk to him. Let him hear your voice." He snorted. "No doubt, a nice change from listening to me." Basil rose and picked up the cup, taking another drink as he walked over to the window. He stretched his back, then massaged his neck with his free hand. "Would you two mind keeping an eye on him while I take a quick shower?" He glanced down at the dark stain on his shirt.

Griffin's blood, thought Katie. She swallowed.

"Of course. Take all the time you need," Lena said. "And try to rest."

Katie wrenched her eyes from Basil's shirt. "And I'm finished with finals, so no school. I can stay all day."

Basil smiled at their willing faces. "Then he's in the best of hands." He checked on Griffin, gave the cover a tug, and left, his tread heavy with weariness.

Lena headed over to Basil's abandoned chair, untying her apron before sitting down with a sigh. Katie folded a leg under her, settling more comfortably.

She frowned to herself, thinking for a moment, then looked over. "Miss Weiss? Why did all this happen? To him? I mean, they're angels, right? Shouldn't they be ... you know... nicer... to each other? Help each other? Not hurt each other?"

Lena pushed up the sleeves of her velour running suit as she pondered the question. "We could say the same thing about people, yes?" she replied, tilting her head to one side. "Terrae Angeli and humans both have free will. The ability to choose between right and wrong. Good and evil." She leaned forward and gazed at the motionless face on the pillow. "Most are like Basil and Griffin. Full of love and light and goodness. So determined to make this world a better place." Lena looked up at the girl.

"And we could say the same thing about people."

ஐ

Basil rubbed his gritty eyes, then checked the clock on the nightstand. By the Light! he grumbled. Why did they let me sleep so long? He rolled off the bed, his bare feet hitting the floor with a thump. Grabbing a clean shirt from the closet, he slipped it on and padded down the hall; he barely missed flattening Katie as she rushed out of Griffin's room.

She squeaked in fright. "Oh, Mr. Raine! I was just coming to ... he woke up! For a few seconds."

Basil pushed past her into the room. Stepping over to the bed, he pressed the back of his fingers against Griffin's cheek. "He's warmer, thank heaven." He eased himself down on the side of the bed. "Fin?"

Griffin's lips twitched. His left eye fluttered opened, then shut again. It opened once more and stared blankly; his right eye was swollen shut.

"Why, hello there, lad," said Basil. "We were wondering when you would join us." He leaned closer as Griffin murmured something. "Beg pardon?"

"Thir see," Griffin repeated, his voice a puff of air.

"Katie, go downstairs and fetch some water, please. Lukewarm. And where the drinking straws are located, I have no idea. Where's Lena?"

"She's making lunch. Be right back." She shot out of the room, her feet thudding on the steps.

Griffin blinked and licked his dry lips as Basil checked his bandages. "Katie's getting some water for you."

"Ka-ee 'ear?"

"Of course she's here. And so's Miss Lena. Your fan club."

Griffin huffed out a breath, a corner of his mouth twitching. He winced at his sore ribs as he tried to push the covers off his shoulders and chest.

"Are you getting too warm?" At Griffin's nod, Basil stood up and folded the comforter back as Lena and Katie hurried into the room. Griffin brightened at the sight of both of them.

"Hey, you," Katie murmured. "Want some water?" She hovered close, helping him with the straw. After a few sips, he settled back and grinned groggily at her as she resumed her perch on the edge of the bed.

"How are you feeling, liebling?" asked Lena. She walked around to the chair and dragged it closer before sitting down.

"Menee erts."

Both woman and girl looked questioningly at Basil, standing by the foot of the bed. "*My knee hurts,*" he translated. Their heads swiveled back to the patient.

"Um-ma aye stuh," he whispered.

"*And my eye's stuck.*" Basil chuckled. "I think he means he can't open it."

"Erts masigh tuh taw."

Lena frowned. Katie bit her lip. Their mouths moved silently as they tried a hand at deciphering.

After a moment, the older woman sat up straight. "I have it!" she announced. "*Hurts my side to talk.*"

Basil bowed his head. "You are now fluent in ... *Fin-ish.*"

All three groaned.

ꙮ

With the dishwasher swishing away in the background, Basil snapped off the lights in the kitchen, rolled down the sleeves of his shirt and made his way through the dark house. After a detour by way of the study to grab a file, he tiptoed upstairs to Griffin's room and paused in the doorway.

"M'awake," called a sleepy voice. Griffin rolled his head as Basil sauntered in. "Did everyone go home already?"

Basil walked over to the desk and dug through the drawer. "Yes, about mid-afternoon." Locating a pen, he opened the file and flipped through several papers before pulling one out. "I assume this is the form I'm supposed to use. I swear, they change these things every century," he grumbled. Still studying it, he ambled over to the bed and sat down. Using the folder as an impromptu table, he checked off several boxes, pressing down firmly on the paper. "Tiro Griffin. Proelium. Winter solstice. 2010 A.D. North America. Passed," he said as he wrote, then signed it with a flourish. "There! I've been waiting three years to do that."

"How many times is this for you? Twenty-two?"

"Twenty-three, actually," said Basil, placing the paper back inside the file. "And I've never been more proud of any of my Tiros than I am of you, lad." He smiled. "I'll let you in on a little secret. Just between you and me." The Mentor lowered his voice. "You've been my favorite, Fin."

Griffin whispered back. "Yeah. You, too, Basil. You've been my favorite Mentor."

They looked at each other for a moment, and then burst out laughing.

Chapter Thirty-One

"Basil, I'm dying down here!"

"Yes, yes. Dying. Jolly good," murmured his Mentor, immersed in his newspaper, one foot propped on the coffee table. "Let's have ten more, eh?"

Griffin rolled his eyes, his face flushed. With a grunt, he raised his injured leg into the air, flexing it to his chest before lowering it back down. "There," he said with a gasp after the obligatory set. "That's thirty total." Panting, he looked up from his position on the living room floor. "So can I go now?" As he waited for the all clear, he flicked a finger at the hearth, sending sparks popping and dancing along the logs. He jumped when Basil cleared his throat in warning.

"And just what are you doing?" Basil frowned over the top of the paper. "I distinctly said no Elements for another week." He hid a smile as Griffin pasted on his best wide-eyed innocent expression. "Oh, for heaven's sake, go." Basil waved a hand in dismissal and buried himself in the world affairs section. "Oh, and Fin? A little less Axe spray, please."

No way, Griffin thought, clambering to his feet. Katie *likes* the way I smell. He hurried upstairs, showered and changed, glancing out his window at Katie's as he tugged a hoodie over his head. He grinned to see her blinds drawn halfway up at a crooked angle. "Coming as quick as I can," he muttered, tying his shoes. He trotted back downstairs, reminding himself to limp as he approached the archway.

"Can I take the car?" He patted his leg. "My knee, you know."

"*May* I take the car."

"May I take the car?" he asked again, gritting his teeth.

"No," said Basil with a broad grin. "A gentle stroll is just the ticket."

He does that every time! "Fine," he grumbled as he slung on his puffy vest, pulling his hood free.

Basil glanced up, checking the time on the mantel clock. "*One* coffee. Decaf."

"Got it. I'll be back by dark." Griffin hurried out the front door into the afternoon sun; the snow crunched underfoot as he walked. As he reached the far sidewalk, the Heflins' front door opened. Bear shot out. Spotting Griffin, he gave a joyful woof and lunged down the steps toward him, Lewis losing the battle on the other end of the leash.

Griffin froze in the middle of the pathway. "Do you have him, Mr. Heflin?"

"Bear. Sit," ordered Lewis, finally bringing the wolfhound under control. He pushed the dog into position. "There! I think it's safe now."

Griffin approached cautiously. Bear whined with eagerness, his massive tail sweeping the snow behind him. "Hey, big guy." He ruffled the dog's ears and ran a hand down his head and neck. "Good boy, Bear."

"Helen and I are taking him for a walk. I need a break from grading all those exams," Lewis said, tugging on his gloves. "Don't ever become a professor, Griffin. You'll spend every winter break scoring—" He stopped, and then they looked at each other, Lewis blushing slightly. "No doubt, you've a different career plan in mind."

"Yeah, you might say that." His grin lit up his entire face.

"Hello, Griffin!" Helen stepped out, zipping up her jacket as she joined them. She looked closely at his face. "Goodness, your eye certainly looks better already. You weren't kidding when you said Terrae Angeli heal so quickly. How's the ribs and knee?"

"All good. Knee's just a little sore, that's all." He gave the dog another pat. "But thanks for holding Bear, Mr. Heflin."

"Well, we better go before our problem child can't behave any longer," said Helen. "The other one is in the kitchen. Go on in." With a wave, they strolled down the street, Bear straining on the leash.

Griffin watched them walk away. He smiled when he saw them reach out and take each other's hand, then he turned and headed for the house. Glancing at the stone angel by the foot of the steps, he saw steam rising from its head and wings in the warmth of the sun. The snow had been swept clear in front of it. He paused and stooped to read the words newly chiseled into its wide base.

> *"The angels keep their ancient places—*
> *Turn but a stone and start a wing!*
> *'Tis ye, 'tis your estrangèd faces,*
> *That miss the many-splendored thing."*

"Amen," he whispered.

ꕥ

"Grab us a spot. I'll get our order," said Katie. "No—I mean it." she added when Griffin started to protest. "Go sit down and rest your knee!" She pushed him toward the tables near the windows.

Should I tell her it's feeling better already? he thought. Smiling to himself, he wound his way through the crowd. Nah. He picked a seat with a view of the street, its lampposts still entwined with post-holiday evergreens. Sunlight and students on break filled the coffee shop with a buzz of energy. As he waited, he cupped a hand in the pool of light, the warmth ancient and familiar at the same time. Idly, he looked up and then sighed, watching with resignation as a redheaded figure bounced through the door.

Spotting her friend at the counter, Carlee rushed over with a squeal. Katie nodded a welcome, and then gestured toward Griffin. As the redhead turned around and waved, Katie mouthed behind her: *Sorry.* Griffin shrugged. After a few minutes, both girls made their way over, steaming drinks in hand, and joined him.

"Hi, Griffin!" Carlee plopped down across from him, pulled the lid off her cup and took a sip. "Hey, how did you get that black eye?" As he opened his mouth, she plowed on. "My brother got a black eye last month. He hit it on the door. Well, he didn't hit it. I slammed the door on him. But it was actually the doorknob that hit him. Is that what happened to you?" He tried again to explain. "Mom was pissed," continued Carlee, apparently able to live without oxygen. "She said I was his big sister and had to watch out for him. Then I got in trouble for telling her I never wanted a little brother. A little brother is one brother too many! Speaking of Mom, I better go. She's in the car." She hopped up, cup in hand. "I'll call you later, Katie. 'Bye, Griffin!"

They watched her dart out the door, and then looked at each other. "Carlee is a... a..." Katie trailed off.

"... a force of nature," finished Griffin. He leaned over his cup, inhaling its black aroma, then picked it up and chugged the scalding liquid in a single gulp. As he slammed the empty cup on the table, Katie stared at him in disbelief.

"How do you *do* that?" she asked, sipping her own coffee cautiously. Before he could answer, she snorted. "Like I have to ask."

He laughed and glanced outside. "Look, it's too nice to be inside," he said, standing up. "I got an idea. Come on." He held out his hand.

"Let me guess," Katie said, jumping up and grabbing her cup. "Swing?"

"Oh, yeah," responded Griffin, his eyes crinkling at the corners.

ꝏ

"What's the deal with the screaming?" Griffin asked, pointing to the little boy clambering over the jungle gym. As he watched, the child launched himself, with a shriek of joy, down the slide to his mother waiting at the bottom. "Fire! The kid's voice could shatter glass!" He sank down on top of a picnic table, resting his feet on the bench.

"Oh, he's just excited." Tossing her empty cup in a nearby trashcan, Katie joined Griffin, grateful for his warmth as he wrapped his arm around her waist. "You know how it was when you were little. And you tried stuff for the first time."

"I was never that little," he said without thinking, his eyes wistful.

"What do you mean?"

"What? Oh, I just meant that I was never a little kid." He nodded toward the toddler. "Not like him."

"Okay. You totally lost me. Of course you were young. I mean, at some point. Right?"

He hesitated. "Um ... remember when I told you that Terrae Angeli are created, not birthed? Well, when we come into being, we're already about ten years old. Both physically and mentally. Give or take a few months."

"You're kidding!" Her mouth sagged. "You mean, you've only been around, on Earth, for ...?"

He nodded. "Yup. Six years. I age about the same rate as you do. Until I reach adulthood. Then I'll slow down. The older I get, the slower I'll age."

Katie took his hand and squeezed it. "Ten, huh? So that's when you went to live with Nicopolis?"

He studied the toes of his shoes. "Yeah." A faint smile crept across his face. "Until I was thirteen. And met Basil." Twisting sideways, he wrapped both arms around her. "And then later I met you." He pulled her close, resting his forehead against hers. "How did I get so lucky?"

"Don't think it was luck."

ꕥ

"Sorry I'm late." Griffin nudged the door closed with his heel as he entered the darkened entryway. "We stopped by the park on the way home." He tossed his vest on the hook and strolled across the hall to the study. "And why are you sitting in the dark?" he asked the figure on the sofa. He leaned over and snapped on the desk lamp, then froze, his stomach lurching at the sight of his Mentor's face. "What's wrong?" he whispered, walking over and sinking down next to him.

Basil reached over and wrapped his hand around Griffin's wrist in a bruising hold, his fingers no longer overlapping as they did three years ago. "Nicopolis..." he choked, staring straight ahead. He stopped, cleared his throat, and tried again. "Nicopolis declared your Proelium a failure, after all." He turned and looked at Griffin.

The fear vying with anger in his Mentor's eyes slammed Griffin's heart against his ribs. "B-but why?"

"The bloody git is now saying that I *threatened* him and that he first lied out of fear. Even after that meeting, Command has decided to believe him," he said in disbelief. "Two Guardians are already on their way." He let go and dragged a hand down his face; the house creaked around them as they sat in stunned silence.

"But I ... but I broke the circle. I know I did," Griffin said, shaking his head. "Can I talk to them? Tell them what really happened?" They both jumped as a blast of wind rattled the windowpanes.

"Stay put," ordered Basil. He rose and clicked off the lamp, then crept out of the study and across the hall to the shadowy living room. Keeping to one side, he peeked around the open drapes, scanning the porch and front yard; as he watched, two figures appeared, the snow eddying around their feet. One towered over the other. Basil's eyes narrowed. He stared for a moment, and then gave a low whistle through his teeth; a rustle and Griffin stood behind him. After glancing once more at the motionless angels outside, he turned and gripped his Tiro's shoulders.

"Listen to me. No, listen! We don't have time. I want you to go upstairs, find my wallet and take the cash. And your cell." He tightened his grip. "Understand?" Griffin nodded, wide-eyed.

Basil clenched his jaw at the old gesture. "Go out my window and head downtown. Do *not*, under any circumstance, contact Lena.

They'll be expecting that." He let go and twisted around, checking out the window. "Good. They're still there."

"What do I..?"

"Stay with the crowds. They won't try anything around so many mortals. Mingle with people until I catch up with you," he said over his shoulder. "Now go."

And Godspeed, son.

Griffin whirled around, snagging his vest from the hall before bolting upstairs. Dashing into his Mentor's bedroom, he felt the house shudder; the front door crashed open as Basil shouted something. He found the wallet and grabbed the bills, stuffing them into his pocket. Hurrying to the window, he peered out at the backyard. All clear. Holding his breath, he eased the sash up, grimacing as it screeched in protest. He squeezed through, gripping the frame to keep from sliding down the roof as he checked the empty yard once more, and then paused, preparing for flight.

An enormous hand clamped around his wrist. Griffin gasped, his feet skittering against the shingles as he struggled to pull free. "I don't think so," a voice boomed. Another hand reached out and grabbed him under the arms, hauling him back inside. "You're as quick as a jackrabbit—I'll give you that," remarked the voice, the speaker hidden in the darkness of the room. "Just what I'd expect from one of Basil's."

"Who are you?" Griffin panted. "Where's Basil?" He squinted, peering up at the huge form as he tried to make out the features.

"Guardian Sukalli. And your Mentor's downstairs. With Guardian Mayla."

A hand gripped his shoulder, spun him around and pushed him out the door. They headed downstairs, Sukalli's cowboy boots punishing the wooden steps. Griffin tried to shrug free; he winced when the Guardian dug his fingers into his shoulder and gave him a shake.

"You just settle down, pup."

Reaching the wedge of light spilling from the living room, Griffin could hear voices raised in anger, Basil's among them. The Guardian prodded him through the archway.

Basil stood by the front windows, his face a storm cloud as he glared across the room. "Mayla, this is ludicrous! Remember our meeting three years ago with Nicopolis? Can't you see what's going on here?"

"Basil, don't you think this is difficult for me? To have to do this to Griffin and to you?" said a soft but stern voice. As Griffin watched, Guardian Mayla rose from the chair near the fireplace. "Hello, Griffin," she said, studying him with a look of sorrow on her face. "I must say, I was stunned when I heard you had failed. Reports indicate that you are a capable Tiro, with numerous successful missions ..." She shook her head, faltering. "I am sorry."

"Nicopolis is lying. You know how he is, Mayla," Basil tried again, pulling Griffin over to his side. "He hates Fin. And me. He's found a way to retaliate. To get back at both of us in one move." He looked at Sukalli, then back at Mayla. "I can't believe Command refuses to even investigate before... before *destroying* Griffin!"

"I agree with you, Basil. Nicopolis can be a vindictive little cuss," interrupted Sukalli. "Heck, we've known *that* since we were all Tiros. But I doubt even Nicopolis would lie about something as ancient and sacred as the Proelium." As the Guardian spoke from his position near the archway, Griffin stared at him. A hawk feather dangled from his ebony ponytail and a small leather pouch hung around his neck by a thong; its decorative beading matched the trim on his fringed buckskin jacket. "Listen, brother," he continued. "I know how you feel—you're trying to protect your apprentice. And I would have done the same when I was a Mentor." He took a step toward them, his bronze face full of sympathy. "But the law is the law."

Mayla nodded in agreement. She straightened and lifted her chin. "Tiro Griffin," she declared formally, "by failing your Proelium, you have shown yourself unfit for duty as a Terrae Angelus. According to our edicts, you must become mortal and live as a human until death takes you." She started toward him.

"No!" With a roar, Basil pushed Griffin into a corner. "Stay down!" he shouted and swung his hand around. Wind blasted through the room, books and papers whirling in a tornado as the drapes flapped wildly, knocking the lamp over. In the darkness, Mayla flung up her arm, protecting her face as she barked an order.

Sukalli planted his feet and raised his hand, palm out. "Sorry, my brother," he shouted over the din. With a sudden jerk, Basil flew backward and smashed through the window, landing on the porch; the Guardian followed, leaping through the opening.

As the wind died down, Griffin scrambled to his feet and bolted toward the gap. "Basil" he cried, his shoes crunching on shattered glass as he reached for the splintered frame.

Mayla sprang forward and grabbed his arm, whipping him around. Holding tightly, she slapped her hand against his chest. "Forgive me," she whispered.

Pain ripped Griffin apart, a white-hot agony that shredded his body and soul into pieces. He screamed, arching backward, and then collapsed. His fingernails tore at the rug as he jerked uncontrollably, his heels drumming against the floor. A flickering blackness engulfed his vision as the torture increased. The pain became a crushing weight.

Mortality.

Chapter Thirty-Two

THE WIND MOANED THROUGH the shattered window and across the empty room, chilling Griffin as he shook under the relentless pain. Bones creaked as his joints pulled open from mortality's weight, and then eased back into position, adjusting. Each breath seemed to crack another rib; tendons stretched and organs labored. Griffin felt himself sinking further, trembling with the anticipation of his heart finally ceasing its insistent pounding. Oh, please. Hurry up and stop beating already, he thought, his eyes squeezed shut. Just stop and let me die. He smiled to himself in relief as his pulse slowed, with longer and longer intervals between each beat.

Then ceased.

A darkness deeper than night pulled him down.

He gasped in shock as a hand suddenly flattened itself against his chest; his heart started up again with an irritated thump. Light poured into Griffin's body, into his soul, and drew him back.

"Oh, no, you don't, lad," said a voice close to his ear. "I'm not letting you slip away that easily."

"B-Basil?" The whisper ghosted past Griffin's lips.

"Fin," Basil whispered back.

A warm droplet splashed on Griffin's face. Summoning all his strength, he pried open his eyelids and looked up at the angel kneeling next to him. "Please?"

"No." Basil blinked as another tear slid down his face, mingling with blood from a gash along his cheekbone; his hand remained splayed across Griffin's chest as Might flowed from Mentor to Tiro.

"Please let me go." *Let me die.*

"Not bloody likely."

A corner of Griffin's mouth twitched. "Promise?" he breathed.

"I promise."

Epilogue

"HAPPY NEW YEAR," whispered Katie, gazing down at Griffin's motionless face as he lay curled on his side, his head pillowed in her lap. She untangled her hand from his, then grabbed the remote and turned off the television, silencing the shrill voice announcing another year's birth. Darkness enveloped the living room. She looked up as a tall figure appeared in the archway.

"Is he asleep?"

"Yeah. I guess watching the ball drop in Times Square wasn't all that exciting."

Basil shrugged. "Well, certainly not on TV." He walked over to the sofa and patted Griffin's leg. "Wake up, Sleeping Ugly."

"Funny," said a raspy voice. "And anyway, I wasn't asleep. I was just ... meditating. Really deeply." Griffin rolled over on his back, blinking up at Katie. "What time is it?" he asked, yawning.

"Time for you to get off of me so I can go home. Mom wants me back by midnight." Katie paused and looked at her watch, "and I'm two minutes late already."

Griffin grunted and sat up, scrubbing a hand through his hair. "I'll walk you home," he said and pushed off the sofa. He staggered a step, banging his shin on the coffee table. "Ow!"

Hopping up, Katie brushed past him and headed toward the entryway. "No way—you're still supposed to be taking it easy," she said, sticking her feet into her fleece boots. She smiled as Griffin joined her, taking her jacket from the hallway hook and helping her on with it. "I'll see you tomorrow," she said, giving him a hug. "Sleep well." She turned and opened the door, slipping out. Trotting down the steps, she glanced back over her shoulder and grinned. "You're going to watch me all the way home, aren't you?" she called up to him.

He shrugged as he slouched in the doorway, his hands stuffed in his pockets. "You can't blame me—it's a nice view," he said. He chuckled when she sauntered off, swinging her hips a few times before breaking into a jog and crossing the street. She waved once more from her front door, then hurried inside. Griffin sighed, then closed and locked the door, leaning wearily against it.

"Fin," called Basil from the living room. "Come join me."

Griffin pushed off and ambled through the archway. A blaze danced in the hearth, illuminating the room, the aroma of burning pine sweetening the air. He flopped down on the sofa and braced his stockinged feet on the edge of the coffee table. "Happy New Year, Basil."

"And to you, lad."

Griffin pointed toward the fireplace. "How did you get the fire started?"

"I employed a centuries-old device," said Basil. He rested his elbows on the arms of the wingback chair, tenting his fingers under his chin.

"What was it?"

"A match."

"Oh, yeah. Those things." Griffin snorted. "Guess I was used to ... you know ... doing that for you." He stared into the flames for a while, feeling Basil's eyes on him. Clearing his throat, he asked in a low voice, "Am I going to make it?"

"Yup."

"How do you know?"

Basil smiled. "Because I know Griffin," he said. "And nothing keeps him down for long. He will rise again." He glanced at the clock on the mantel and then stood. "Well, I'm off to bed. Don't stay up too late, eh?"

Griffin nodded, his gaze fixed on the hearth as Basil left the room. He sank further into the cushions and leaned his head back, watching the reflection from the firelight skip along the beams.

I should go to bed, too, he thought, but I'm too tired to even get off this sofa! Basil says I'll eventually get used to it. I hope so. Because it's hell right now. How do mortals do it? Live with this constant burden? All this weight? I never realized how trapped humans were by their humanity. Until I became one.

Katie's been awesome. I'm glad she doesn't make me talk about it. She just sits beside me. Sometimes, it's all I can do to hang on to her hand.

I wish I knew what's going to happen to me next. Basil tells me not to worry. That nothing's changed between us and to trust that we'll get through all this. To keep the faith.

Guess it's all I can do.

Lowering his head, he watched as the blaze ebbed away and sputtered out; the glowing coals slowly dimmed. "I know how you feel," he murmured to the embers. With a groan, he shoved off the cushion, catching the arm of the sofa for balance, then shuffled toward the hall.

As he left the room and made his way up the stairs, Fire suddenly flared back to life in the hearth behind him.

A promise in the dark.

Author's Note

In the summer of 2009, I came across an obscure and rather brief description from the Middle Ages about a lower caste of angels. According to Catholic tradition, these angels, besides acting as guardians of humankind, were also said to control the four elements of earth, fire, wind, and water. And thus, Griffin, Basil, and the other Terrae Angeli were born.

Elaborating on the idea of an angelic chain of command, the fictitious Kellsfarne Manuscript gives a nod to the early Christian writing *The Celestial Hierarchy*, which is a work from the fifth century that influenced Thomas Aquinas, a medieval Catholic priest and theologian who divided angels into a pecking order, so to speak, based on their proximity to God.

However, the belief in supernatural or angelic beings can be found in many of the world's religions and is not limited to Christianity. I borrowed from Judaism as well as Islam, Hinduism, and ancient Babylon; for example, *Sukalli* is a Babylonian term meaning *angel* or *messenger.*

And to emphasize the antiquity of the Terrae Angeli, I used the Latin phrase, *Tiro,* as a synonym for *apprentice* or *young recruit* just as *Proelium* is Latin for *battle.*

In addition to religious influences, I've also added bits and pieces from other cultures and historical events. Touches of classical Sparta, the Irish myths of Cuchulainn, Finn and the Red Branch, the European feudal system, the Plains Indians of North America, and Great Britain's Royal Air Force during World War Two all found their way into Griffin's tale.

The lines inscribed on the base of the Heflins' stone angel are from a poem entitled *The Kingdom of God.* It was written by the English poet, Francis Thompson (1859-1907).

Acknowledgments

I would like to thank the following people: My mother, Louise M., who first loved Griffin; Stephanie M., who first loved Basil; Kaci G. (book lover and librarian extraordinaire) for on-going support and enthusiasm; Kelly A. (my sister); Lee G. and Derek G. (my brothers) for their shrewd observations and suggestions; to my editor, Robina Williams, whose expertise in Latin was a serendipitous blessing; to Ardy M. Scott for cover art that took my breath away; and to my publisher, Lida E. Quillen, for giving Griffin wings.

I would also like to thank the following stars for creating such amazing book trailers: James B. Gerald B. Cameron B., Katherine B., David D., Dane F., Timothy H., Zachary K., Kyle M., Katherine M., Mitchel P., Nathan P., Jared R., Matthew V., Hailey V., Mitchell W., Alexander W., and Mr Milliron.

About the author

All her life, the archetypal hero and his journey have enthralled Darby Karchut. A native of New Mexico, Darby grew up in a family that venerated books and she spent her childhood devouring one fantasy novel after another. Fascinated by mythologies from around the world, she attended the University of New Mexico, graduating with a degree in anthropology. After moving to Colorado, she then earned a Master's in education and became a social studies teacher.

Drawing from her extensive knowledge of world cultures, she blends ancient myths with modern urban life to write stories that relate to young teens today.

Darby is a member of the Society of Children's Book Writers and Illustrators and the Pikes Peak Writers Guild. She lives in Colorado Springs, Colorado with her husband, where she still teaches at a local junior high school. She enjoys running, biking, and skiing the Rocky Mountains in all types of weather.

Griffin Rising is her first novel. She is currently working on the sequel, *Griffin's Fire.*

For book group discussion questions and more information about the author, visit http://www.darbykarchut.com

Don't miss any of these
other exciting SF/F books

Angelos
(1-933353-60-0, $16.95 US)

Caves, Cannons and Crinolines
(1-60619-112-8, $14.95 US)

Dragon's Moon
(1-933353-53-8, $14.95 US)

Gaea
(1-60619-183-7, $18.95 US)

Infinite Space, Infinite God
(1-933353-62-7, $18.95 US)

Jerome and the Seraph
(1-931201-54-4, $15.50 US)

Nine Lives and Three Wishes
(1-933353-55-4, $13.50 US)

Valley of the Raven
(1-933353-75-9, $16.95 US)

You, Me, Naideen and a Bee
(1-60619-208-6, $19.95 US)

Twilight Times Books
Kingsport, Tennessee

Order Form

If not available from your local bookstore or favorite online bookstore, send this coupon and a check or money order for the retail price plus $3.50 s&h to Twilight Times Books, Dept. LS611 POB 3340 Kingsport TN 37664. Delivery may take up to two weeks.

Name: ______________________________

Address: ____________________________

____

Email: ______________________________

I have enclosed a check or money order in the amount of

$__________

for ______________________________________ .

Griffin's Fire
by Darby Karchut

Coming April 2012 from
Twilight Times Books

Struggling to adjust to life as a teen mortal, ex-angel Griffin enrolls in high school, which quickly proves to be a battleground. And to make matters worse, his Mentor, Basil, has been ordered to take on a new apprentice, the gifted and egotistical seventeen-year-old Sergei, who is determined to make Griffin's life a nightmare.

But secrets, even kept for the best of reasons, can break hearts and Griffin is forced to make a choice that could cost him Basil's trust and Katie's love.

If you enjoyed this book, please post a review
at your favorite online bookstore.

Twilight Times Books
P O Box 3340
Kingsport, TN 37664
Phone/Fax: 423-323-0183
www.twilighttimesbooks.com/

CPSIA information can be obtained at www.ICGtesting.com
233211LV00004B/33/P